The Princess in My Head

J. G. Matheny

Aignos Publishing
an imprint of Savant Books and Publications
Honolulu, HI, USA
2018

Published in the USA by Aignos Publishing LLC
An imprint of Savant Books and Publications LLC
2630 Kapiolani Blvd #1601
Honolulu, HI 96826
http://www.aignospublishing.com

Printed in the USA

Edited by Karen Grimshaw/Michael Davis
Cover by Sydney Dean

13 digit ISBN: 978-0-9963255-7-8

First Edition: June 2018
Library of Congress Control Number: 2018908747

Dedication

To Kelley

PART I
The Novel

J. G. Matheny

Chapter One

Present day

Good evening, loyal subjects. Princess Allison the Benevolent *here, checking in for my nightly webcast.*

For starters, let me apologize for what I understand is our seventh solid day of rain in a row. It's hard to behave nobly when you're slipping and falling in the mud. Or it splashes up from your bike's back tire making a skunk stripe from your pants up your t-shirt. Or it tracks into your humble homes making your moms yell. If I could change the weather, you know that I would. *My only wish is for my loyal subjects to enjoy life as much as possible. Might I suggest that everyone buy a pair of those great rubbery shoes known as* Gators? *Not only will they protect your loyal feet better, they come in such wonderful colors like green, orange, pink and purple. And since they're made from an oil resin form of rubber—I looked that up—they wash up quickly and easily in a tub of water.*

Before I sign off, I am taking a poll. Today is Wednesday, *a day and a word that I love. But* Thursday *is not my favorite and I am considering issuing a royal edict changing its name to something more interesting. Please feel free to submit your suggestions as I will offer a prize to whoever is the cleverest. That's it for now. Princess Allison the Benevolent signing off.*

"Allison! Bonita is here!" Mom yelled.

Bonita waited for me at the bottom of the stairs, trying awkwardly to keep her balance and fit her muddy *Nikes* on the terribly insufficient mat the Queen Mother refers to as our foyer rug. My brother's *Gators* took up space, but it was an enormous, unfamiliar pair of brown *Sorrel* boots that presented the challenge. Bonita is a true loyal subject. She would rather fall over on her butt than step off the mat and mess up my floor.

"Lady Bonita. Welcome loyal subject," I said. This is our standard greeting.

"Princess Allison," Bonita said with a little rehearsed bow—her standard response. "Am I too late for the webcast?"

I swung around the banister and landed next to her on the hardwood floor, almost slipping in my striped socks.

"Yup. Sorry. Mom had me hurry. She's got a date tonight."

Bonita's name means *pretty* in Spanish. Reality falls a little short, however, which is a state of affairs that isn't lost on Bonita. That's probably why she was my most eager recruit as a lady in waiting.

As my most loyal helper, I appreciate the beauty of her soul, and don't get hung up on the things her mom and dad always harp on—the roll of tubbiness around her middle and the slightly imperfect teeth. They're holding braces hostage right now until she loses weight. I think that's a terrible thing to do to an adolescent. After all, we're going through the dreaded puberty and we're all a little messed up. Can't they show a little compassion? Maybe straight teeth are just the encouragement she needs to take care of the other perceived shortcomings.

Anyway, as *Princess Allison the Benevolent*, I figure it's my job to take up the slack and make her feel at least as beautiful as her name.

"Did you have an item for discussion?" I asked.

"Not really. I was just thinking we could start our list of weekend activities that don't involve TV," Bonita said, still trying to keep her balance.

Bonita is positively obsessed with getting children away from TV sets. If she grows up to be a presidential candidate, no doubt that issue will top her political platform.

"Good idea," I said. "We'll do that on tomorrow night's webcast. I talked about muddy feet tonight."

Bonita giggled. It was actually a half laugh that's a little high pitched—like a trill you do on the top end of the piano. I like it. It's part of what makes Bonita, well...Bonita.

"If you'll pardon the affront, *Princess Allison*," Bonita said— her standard words to signal she planned to disagree with me, "but don't you think that topic's a little *lame*?"

"Maybe. But look at what you're doing just to keep your feet off my floor. You were gonna fall over and maybe hurt yourself. I think muddy feet are on every kid's mind right now. Take your shoes off. I'll move the boots. They don't belong here."

"Whose are they?" Bonita asked as she shuffled her *Nikes* carefully into a small pile.

I scrunched my nose and shook my head. "Haven't the foggiest. But from the size of them, we should call the newspaper. Tell 'em

Bigfoot's been sighted in LaPoste, Wisconsin."

I stared too long at the big boots. Whose were they? And where was the gigantic person that owned them? Wandering somewhere through my house?

"Allison?"

"Oh yeah, are you hungry?"

"Maybe. A little," Bonita replied.

I stared at her expression. Bonita's top lip was curled under while the bottom lip still smiled up. To an outsider, she looked goofy, but I knew she was just thinking what to say next. I helped her out.

"Noodles and applesauce again?"

Bonita nodded.

"For *dinner*? You need some protein, Loyal Subject! Doesn't your mom understand the food pyramid?"

Bonita shuffled after me into our fairly adequate kitchen. The townhouse is small but the kitchen belongs in a farmhouse in Vermont. We have tall oak cabinets and a white tile countertop, and a huge island right in the middle where we eat and throw everything—like my homework, mom's laptop, mail from the past century, the fruit bowl—that doesn't belong somewhere else…

I headed to the pantry closet and hefted the giant *Peter Pan* jar to the counter. From the frig I grabbed celery Mom had placed in a water pitcher to crisp. Bonita dug the stalk in ravenously.

Sucking the peanut butter from the roof of her mouth, Bonita said, "Remember when you covered it in your webcast two months ago? The food pyramid, I mean? I printed it out and left it on the counter for my mom. But I guess she didn't notice. I think my mother wants to starve me. She says noodles will fill me up and I won't eat as much other stuff."

"My loyal subjects are being starved to death! And their oppressors are right under the same roof! How *tragic*. We need to repeat the broadcast. Should I make protein an edict?" I asked.

Bonita shrugged. "Edicts confuse me. What if they're not followed?"

She was right. Every good ruler knows the power of a good edict. These are the laws loyal subjects must follow. But too many edicts can bring down a monarchy.

"You're right. If edicts aren't followed, then punishment is called for. But I'm Princess Allison the *Benevolent*. Punishing subjects isn't my thing. Maybe I'll just word my message strongly and then repeat it more often. Let's schedule the food pyramid again for next Monday's program. Make sure your mom tunes in."

Bonita grabbed a pencil lying on the counter, and tore the top from a cereal box. She scribbled the note.

"I wish you could issue an edict on Sophia and her *pack*. Man, they make my life miserable," Bonita said as she pocketed the note.

"You said they've been leaving you alone lately. What happened?"

Sophia is considered by some weakling souls to be the coolest girl in school. I know better since we used to be best friends millions of years ago. Her *pack* is everyone's name for the girls who mindlessly follow her around.

Bonita made another face.

"They have been, except for today in gym. You know I can't climb that rope. I was horrified Miss Amherst made me try. She's usually on my side. But I guess there's this fitness test that everyone in the school has to take and, well, I tried. I got up a little far. It wasn't that bad, really, until Sophia started laughing at me. I really hate her. She thinks that just because she has long hair and her mom lets her highlight it so it looks blonde, that she's better than everyone. Then Haley started in too, and you know the boys just follow along because they're so stupid. So I was stuck on this rope. I was afraid to go down because now everyone was staring, and my gym shorts had made a big wedgie..."

"I *hate* it when that happens. So what did you do?" I asked.

"Well, I was ready to just open my fists and drop down to the mat, but I was afraid I'd sprain an ankle..."

"Sophia can be so mean..."

"Yeah...you know that better than anybody. But then Richie Harrell—he was next in line—farted quite loudly and everyone laughed. In the confusion, I kind of wiggled down. When it was his turn, he kept farting really loud all the way up the rope and everyone went crazy. Can you imagine? I think he was doing it on purpose to get attention. Anyway, they forgot about me and my wedgie. How'd you do?"

Bonita has gym third period with the entire seventh grade popular unit. I don't have it until fifth period. I'm lucky. All the kids in my class are nice.

"Oh, you know..."

"What? Did you set another school record? Did you make it to the top in like...five seconds?"

I'm actually pretty good at gym and I have set a couple stupid, little school records. Like, I can do the most push-ups for a girl. I can't help it. I'm just athletic. But as a benevolent princess, I simply can't act stuck up about something as silly as gym.

"I don't know. I just went up and down and that was it. Let's get upstairs. I'll burn you a copy of tonight's webcast and we can pick some topics for tomorrow. I'm thinking of changing the name for Thursday."

Bonita and I headed for the stairs. I eyed her muddy *Nikes* as we passed the landing.

"Why don't you get some *Gators*?" I asked.

J. G. Matheny

Chapter Two

The Renaissance

Welcome loyal subjects to today's proclamation. On this wonderful April day in the year of Our Lord 1590, Princess Aqualine the Wise wishes you to know about something vitally important that came to me in my royal dream last night. Recall yee my earlier proclamations on our disastrous spring with all its rain and floods? The cold and the chill hath brought fever. Many of my loyal subjects have fought terrible disease. But our plight may be rendered easier if we protect our feet with a brightly colored covering. These coverings can be made of pliable stretchy fabric that keeps the wet out but is also very easy to clean.

I will dub these new items Gators. I know that this is a funny, unfamiliar word, but since the Renaissance spirit now engages us all, why not embrace something new? The bright color is extremely important because the Gators must be made in green, orange, pink and purple. Won't that be lively? And so much more healthful. Before I dip my quill into my berry juice vat to sign off for today, I am also thinking of issuing an edict to change the name for Thursday to another, more beautiful word. As always, your beloved Princess Aqualine the Wise is open to your suggestions on this topic. Good day.

"'Tis so chilly this morning Milady, what with the spring rain falling outside our castle dormer. May I bring your warm jumper?" Lady Bonifay asked, halting her soundless ministering to the fire.

How could the Princess think this a *wonderful April day*? What with the chilly mustiness inside the castle walls? Days like this make *me* miserable and yet the Princess is so cheery, Lady Bonifay thought.

Princess Aqualine stopped writing to gaze out the castle's glazed windows.

"Why yes, I would like my *warm jumper*. I suppose I am rather chilly. But I beseech thee please use its special name. It's a *Snuggly,* remember? I cannot believe I left my cozy mattress to scribble this proclamation but this wonderful idea came to me in the night and I felt I must write it down."

Lady Bonifay smiled. The Princess' enthusiasm was catching. She ambled across the stone floor, cushioned by large woven rugs, to the monstrous wardrobe against the wall. It had once belonged to a king many decades ago and looked regal and imposing. There were hunt scenes carved along its edges with riders on horseback racing from floor to ceiling up its sides. The cabinet opened by pulling on two ornate horse heads.

Lady Bonifay didn't like the horse heads. The wood carver had given them angry expressions and beady eyes. She grasped them valiantly and covered the eyes with her thumbs. Then she gave a powerful yank. The wardrobe doors swung open displaying a rod bearing Princess Aqualine's gowns and a column of shelves.

Naturally it was on the top shelf, Lady Bonifay realized with dismay. Being short and plump, the reach to the higher shelves was a chore. She scooted over a wooden stool, hiked her brocade skirt and climbed up. She reached high with one arm while clutching the wardrobe, careful not to touch any more animal eyes. She pulled out a blue velvet cloak and carefully guided it down.

The fabric was rich and soft. She stood behind Princess Aqualine and held it out in front. Aqualine slipped one arm through a wide sleeve and then the other and hugged the garment around her as Lady Bonifay fastened the back with ties.

"You know, Milady, your warm jumper idea was conceived for winter's cold weather and to sit before the fire, but it works as well in the spring time when the rains seep through the castle walls."

"*Snuggly*," Princess Aqualine corrected again and then sighed. "I know it is an odd name but we must get used to it. And speaking of odd names, please listen to what I've written so far this morning. I have another fine idea but it too comes with an odd name."

Aqualine held up the parchment page she'd been writing on and read aloud to her lady in waiting.

"I wish to know what you think!" she said when finished reading, laying the page back upon the slab table she used as a desk.

Her lady in waiting stood still and gulped.

"I have important ideas on keeping Thursday in its own right but first, if you'll pardon the question, Princess Aqualine, how should your loyal subjects obtain these *Gators*?"

Aqualine looked out the window at the rain and concentrated. She furrowed her brow.

"The idea is an ambitious one, even for you," Lady Bonifay continued.

"Hmmm, you are most right. But I have it! I believe that I should offer a reward to whomever in the kingdom can develop the formula for this new substance. From my dream, I know that it is a resin from a substance we can call *rubber*."

Lady Bonifay frowned. "Once again, Milady if you'll pardon my disagreement. Do you truly think it is worth your subject's time to invent this new substance when it's only purpose would be to make brightly colored foot wear?"

Princess Aqualine shrugged. "I know it sounds a little silly but I feel in my heart that it is truly a very good idea."

"You know the Lady Saraphina will be standing by to make fun. This is just the kind of idea that she will scoff," Bonifay said.

Ah yes, Aqualine remembered. "Such as she did with my *Snuggly*."

"Exactly, Milady. Perhaps we could have embraced the warm jumper, but when you insisted upon calling it a *Snuggly,* that seemed to take us too far. And dost thou remember that the early woolen weavings proved itchy, not snuggly at all." Lady Bonifay scrunched her nose.

Aqualine nodded. She remembered that part. Coming up with just the right fabric proved most difficult. She'd enlisted a number of the kingdom's seamstresses to develop the pattern. One of their early versions was made of furry animal skins sewn together. The garment was warm and snuggly from the *outside* and attracted the castle's puppies and kittens that wanted to curl into its furry warmth, but inside her skin felt oily and itchy from the pelt's tannins. Finally, just when Lady Saraphina's nay-saying was turning the realm's interest away from the *Snuggly*, one seamstress blended silk with wool on a special loom and crafted the perfect velvet.

"But now they are quite popular for sitting before the fire and they've brought such relief during our horrendous rains this spring," Aqualine said.

"I only wish to protect you from ridicule, my princess. Lady Saraphina is popular within the realm with those who wish only to parade their clothes and go to balls. Remember the mean words when you suggested your top of the lap desk?"

"Lap top desk. You have to say the words in that order," Aqualine corrected. "But I truly believe that once we have this new substance, we can use it for many other things that need protection from water and damp: for drier floors, for example, and roofs that don't leak."

Lady Bonifay walked behind and slowly began unwinding Princess Aqualine's long hair from the night braids. She giggled.

"But the castle's roofs don't leak that often. The carpenter fills holes with pitch and it works fairly well. We can walk easily around the entire yard and never get wet. I can carry an umbrella for you when you cross the pathways, and have clean slippers ready for you on the other side. You are a princess after all." She yanked a large section of Aqualine's hair free and brushed it carefully.

"But I must *serve* my people," Aqualine insisted. "Being a princess shouldn't be about privilege. It should be about responsibility. I have to take care of my loyal subjects and make their lives easier. "

J. G. Matheny

Chapter Three

Present day

Bonita crawled onto my bed and pushed aside a pile of clean clothes I had yet to fold.

"If you'll pardon the affront, Princess Allison, but you could be popular like Sophia if you tried. Lots of kids know you. They listen to your webcasts. They think you're really smart and helpful. And if your mom let you grow your hair longer and get your ears pierced..."

I cut her off. "Lady Bonita, I like my hair short. It doesn't flop in my face when I run. If I was popular then I'd spend all my time trying to stay popular and wondering what people think of me and why somebody didn't call me like she said she would, and all that crazy stuff. I have other things on my mind. Like why your mother thinks it's motivational not to feed you."

Bonita hugged my fuzzy *Mr. Teddy Boo* to her chest. She shook her head.

"I suppose. Besides, if you were popular, I probably wouldn't be your friend."

"You'll always be my friend," I said, as I plopped into my tan leather computer chair.

Bonita gave *Mr. Teddy Boo* a squeeze. "You don't want to be popular?" she asked.

"Not if it means I can't do what I want and chose my own friends. That's not fun," I said.

"Yeah, well. Even if I wanted to be popular, which I don't, I couldn't. I'm stuck."

"I disagree. You're probably much more popular than you know. You're Princess Allison's Lady in Waiting and we have lots of kids log onto our webcast. They count more to me than the social group at school."

Lady Bonita thinks she doesn't have the power to be popular and is stuck with her current social standing. I know she is wrong. We disagree.

I watched her as she walked over to my computer. The screen was the biggest and best Dad could find when he bought it for me two years ago. Mom wished he'd just sent me cash for college instead of the fancy computer system, but I don't. Bonita pulled up the response log from the webcast. She scrolled down the page, reading.

"Princess Allison, look! Here's a comment for me! I know this kid. He sits behind me in geography. He wants to know if I can ever be promoted and what you'd make me if I was. It's a good question, but I like being your lady in waiting, and I like you being *Princess Allison*," Bonita said.

"See, what'd I tell you? You're popular with the *right* people," I replied.

I heard knocking on the bedroom door. There's a "Do Not Disturb" sign out there but I don't mean it to be rude and Mom doesn't take it that way. I've actually cautioned my loyal subjects in a webcast titled "Bedroom Privacy Etiquette" to include parents in such signage decisions. My sign signals I might be broadcasting to my loyal subjects. Mom knows to knock quietly when she needs me. My side of the bargain is that I agree to open the door right away when I'm free.

I shuffled the desk chair across the carpet on its wheels and opened the door a tiny bit.

"Hi Honey. We're about to leave for the movie. I wanted you to meet Mike. We were just out on the patio."

She pushed open the door and the biggest human being I've ever seen followed her into my bedroom.

Bonita gasped and crawled back against my headboard, nearly strangling *Mr. Teddy Boo.*

"This is *Mike*," my mother said sweetly, leading him by the hand like he was a captured gorilla or ...well...*Bigfoot.*

His head barely cleared my doorway. The brown leather jacket he wore looked probably nine times the size of my *Limited Too* jacket. His enormous neck crushed his sweater's white turtle neck into a skinny worm roll. But that wasn't the most phenomenal part. He had an amazing red beard!

I knew I was staring. Bonita's mouth had dropped open. *Bigfoot* just laughed.

"You get this reaction a lot, Mike?" Mom asked. She was almost tiny in contrast. Her head barely reached his shoulder, and she was wearing those spikey heeled boots that made her as tall as humanly possible.

"Yeah, it happens. Hi, Allison. Hi, Bonita. Did I hear her call you *Princess* Allison?" *Bigfoot* asked.

Oh great, here it comes. My mother chimed in before I had the chance.

"Yes, Allison is a *Princess* and Bonita is her *Lady in Waiting.* See over there?"

Mom pointed to the computer table.

"She's got her computer set up to do webcasts to her *realm,* which is actually a fair number of kids from school and the neighborhood. Allison, Mike is a police detective."

Mom smiled so goofily up at Mike. He turned to her and raised this big paw to her face. He held her chin in it briefly and Mom was totally mesmerized, staring up at him. It was disgusting.

Bonita corrected loudly, "She's Princess Allison *the Benevolent.*"

Mike didn't notice. He was too busy making goo-goo eyes at my middle-aged mother. Didn't he realize she paid beauty magicians thousands of dollars every year to keep her hair looking blonde, her face wrinkle-free and her nails long?

I said, "Being a Princess isn't about privilege. It's about responsibility."

"She takes care of the loyal subjects in her kingdom," Bonita added.

"Yes, I rule," I said with emphasis. Was he even *listening*?

Mom pushed Mike away playfully and he looked over at me.

"Yeah, I know. *Kids rule,*" Mike said and saluted us with a fist pump.

Mom swung her black leather jacket over her shoulders.

"We'll be home about eleven. We're just doing a quick dinner and movie. You'll be just fine," Mom instructed, not really concerned whether we would be or not.

Mike slid an enormous paw onto my shoulder and patted it. His touch was surprisingly gentle. Then he followed Mom from the room.

We watched as the door closed behind them.

"He doesn't get it," Bonita said, sadly. "He's an amazingly huge man with an important job, but he still doesn't get it."

"Right. I think I'm destined for something pink the next time he comes over. Again."

"All your mom's boyfriends miss the point, don't they?"

I stared at the closed door. They sure did.

Chapter Four
The Renaissance

Lady Bonifay clucked her tongue, and twisted Princess Aqualine's braid. "But *rubber*? That is such an ugly word. Perhaps we should change it, if it is really to become a revolutionary substance."

Princess Aqualine thought about this. Rubber was the word from the princess in her head but it *was* rather awkward. Saying it aloud made her lips pop in an undignified way. And what indeed was being rubbed?

"Hmm. I do not much like the name either. What may we call it? I know it to be a pliable and moldable substance that can be stretched across surfaces to make them waterproof. Perhaps we can call it Molder...ahh, molder pliant? Nay, that name does not sing," Princess Aqualine groaned.

"Or *Stretchy*!" Lady Bonifay said with enthusiasm. She clapped her hands. "Dost thou not see? It will be as your Snuggly name. Only *Stretchy*! It is lyrical!"

"Perchance a more dignified name, Lady Bonifay?"

"Princess Aqualine, you are the clever and wise one. I will leave you to work on its name."

"Actually, Lady Bonifay, although so many give me credit for my clever ideas..."

"Why they call you Aqualine the *Wise*," Bonifay interrupted.

"Ah, yes. I have developed a reputation around the countryside as the *wise little princess*. Finally something to be known for other than the littlest sister to the future king. But I am not that wise. I owe so many of my ideas to the little Princess in my royal dream. When my dream washed over me last night and the puffy clouds parted in my mind, I saw her image so clearly. As though she were on stage and I in her audience. Her hair and costumes are much different. And her means of delivering proclamations is so very odd. But her guidance is remarkable. By the way, what do you think of my changing the name for Thursday? 'Tis a good idea?"

"If thou will pardon the opposition, Princess Aqualine, I doth disagree. I believe Thursday to be the best day in the entire week. It is named for *Thor*, the mythical god of thunder. *Thor* was a giant god with red hair and a flowing beard who protected an entire kingdom. If you take away his day, he just may take away his protection and we really need it in this uncertain time."

Lady Bonifay finished the braid and circled it around Aqualine's head like a wreath. Pinning it tightly, she inserted small flowers among the hair. Aqualine surveyed herself in the mirror.

"What do you suppose I would look like with short hair?" she asked.

"Like *Prince* Aqualine," Lady Bonifay laughed. "Now, let us return the Snuggly to the wardrobe and dress for the day. I will assist you to the town square where we can hang today's proclamation."

She helped the Princess into her ruffled pantaloons and brocade dress.

Aqualine crossed to the desk table where her scrolled proclamation lay. She unrolled it, dipped her quill and carefully crossed out her last paragraph. Thursday would stay as it was.

"We best get this posted!"

J. G. Matheny

Chapter Five

The Present

Good evening loyal subjects. Princess Allison the Benevolent here, checking in for my nightly webcast.

For starters, I am so happy that many of you felt the advice on Gators worthwhile. My blog has registered quite a few comments. Heather from Crescent Street says she wishes there were Gators for dogs. I guess her Lab has made a real mess of the stairway carpet and the Jeep's upholstery. Bummer.

On my other topic from last night—when I proposed changing the name for Thursday? Well, I'm re-thinking this idea. It seems Thursday is named after this amazing warrior god Thor who is known for protecting entire countries and children. Lady Bonita is right now researching more on this subject and will post her report on Thor to our blog later tonight. He is so much more than a Marvel comic. This new information came to me in my dream last night. That reliable, yet strange voice told me that if we remove Thor's day, we might lose his protection. And I think any protection, even mythical, in these uncertain times is a good thing.

My apologies to Ryder from Reed Street who wanted Thursday to be renamed Potterday in honor of his hero Harry Potter. I know that he put a lot of thought into that idea but, oh well. That's it for now. Princess Allison the Benevolent signing off.

Bonita looked up from the library book she'd been studying.

"I think it's important that you admitted you were wrong to change Thursday. *Thor* was such an amazing god! It says here he could bring animals back to life. That's my favorite part. I wish he'd been around for my cat K.C."

Our website roll call said we'd had forty-eight listeners. That was a new record.

Bonita said, "You know, *Thor* reminds me of ..."

"No—don't say it," I cried, pulling my velvet pillow over my face.

"No, Allison. You have to listen. He reminds me of Mike—the guy your mom is dating? Mike is just huge, like *Thor*. And the red beard and hair—whoa! Come on—it occurred to you, too, right? And he's a detective—that's a protector of justice, right? Mike could be a modern-day *Thor.*"

I have to admit the similarity had occurred to me.

"Princess Allison, if you'll pardon the affront, I think you should give Mike a chance. He brought you that cool scarf and the diary today. At least he's trying."

When Bonita and I came home from school today, Mom was making Mike a steak. He gave us one of those 'Kids Rule' fist pumps and pointed to a package on the counter.

"Bonita, the scarf was pink and the diary was covered in blue fuzzy fake fur. They looked like Disney souvenirs from a visit to *The Magic Kingdom*."

Bonita closed the book and returned it to my bookshelf.

"Well, if you'll again pardon the affront, Princess Allison, not everyone has been to Disney World. I haven't. And souvenirs from there sound like something special to me. I happen to like Disney, and I wouldn't mind it if someone bought me a scarf or a diary from their store. And I wouldn't care if it was covered in fur. That seems kind of nice, actually. The only presents I get these days are *Healthy Gourmet* frozen dinners and brochures for fat camp."

I sat up, startled. "Bonita—I'm sorry."

"Allison, sometimes you behave like a princess—and not a noble one. I like being your lady in waiting when you are doing important things, and thinking grand thoughts for the common good, but when you start on about your mother's boyfriends and how they treat you, well, let's just say you're less benevolent in my eyes."

Wow. I hadn't thought about things that way. Was Bonita right?

"Okay. What if Mike is really a modern-day protector in our kingdom?" I asked.

"Then that would make you wrong, and you'd owe him an apology. And you'd have to pledge to be nicer because you might actually need him," Bonita replied, crossing her eyes to punctuate the obvious-ness of the solution.

"But I don't think I need saving and protecting."

"Then maybe he's here to protect your realm. And he's going to fight a battle for us or somebody we know. "

"Hmmm. Maybe," I said. It was certainly worth considering.

J. G. Matheny

Chapter Six
The Renaissance

Princess Aqualine skipped down the castle steps. She hugged the rolled parchment in her right hand, and with her left expertly lifted her skirts. Lady Bonifay trailed behind puffing with the strain of keeping up. It was nigh on eight in the morning and the rain had stopped, although dark clouds still circled the skies.

They stepped lightly over the various puddles and muddy spots in the castle yard and proceeded through the magnificent iron gate into the town square. Men wearing tunics over woolen britches pushed their carts into place for the market selling day. Their tall boots were muddy.

The carts laden with fruits, vegetables, breads, baskets and trinkets would shortly draw a crowd: ladies shopping for today's food, hungry visitors, castle cooks needing provisions. The carts formed a path to the town square and Lady Bonifay ambled after the Princess, trying hard not to be diverted by the pleasant aromas.

"Pray, keep up, Lady Bonifay. We are not yet to St. Timothy's and I fear the mass will end soon. We must be posted before!" Princess Aqualine called over her shoulder.

She continued toward the elegant Church built three hundred years ago, passing the site where the gallows once stood. Princess

Aqualine's mother had torn them down the year she'd been named Queen. Up ahead was the great column constructed of wood and stone, and the tablet upon which the proclamation would be posted.

Lady Bonifay scrambled on and then pulled up short next to Princess Aqualine. Three girls stood watching them from beneath the column.

"Oh, what are you proclaiming today, Princess Aqualine? Another *crazy* idea?" asked the tallest girl. She had long blonde hair the color of corn silk and large eyes. "And look, there is Lady Bonifay following along blindly, as usual."

"Lady Saraphina, you are welcome to challenge my proclamations but not my loyal lady in waiting. You and your *pack* may take your leave if you have nothing happy to say," Princess Aqualine responded.

The tall blond girl sputtered.

"My pack? Pray what is my *pack*, Princess Aqualine? Or might I say *Little Princess Aqua* as many have returned to calling you?" Lady Saraphina asked.

Princess Aqualine felt her cheeks grow hot. Oh no, she thought. I am turning red as a beet in front of Saraphina. Stop it at once, she commanded herself and took a deep breath.

"I am sorry. I don't know from whence that expression came. It just flew to my lips upon its own wings."

Lady Saraphina looked quite pleased with herself.

"If you'll pardon the intrusion, Princess Aqualine, might I speak?" Lady Bonifay asked. She'd been shuttering herself behind a ledge, trying to remain out of view. Lady Saraphina scared her. What with her sharp tongue and pompous manner. But perchance she had gone too far this time.

Lady Bonifay gulped but fire was in her eyes. "Yes, your *pack*. Alone you are each like a castle pet, quiet and companionable and able to do little harm. But together you are as a pack of dogs, barking loudly and wreaking havoc."

Saraphina's eyes grew wide with surprise. One of her girls giggled. Then Saraphina shrugged her shoulders and leaned in to read as Princess Aqualine posted the parchment.

"You believe someone in this kingdom should develop this ugly thing you call *rubber* and adapt it for garish shoes? What a waste of our time. Why don't you plan a ball instead? Something fun that your loyal subjects will enjoy?"

The girls joined hands and began to circle Princess Aqualine and Lady Bonifay, laughing and dancing in step.

"Yes, something fun!" one girl cried.

"But being a princess isn't always about throwing balls and having great fun. I must lead my loyal subjects!" Aqualine insisted, but now she was smiling. A ball would be fun.

"She must *rule*," Lady Bonifay agreed.

"Princess Aqualine *Rules*!" a deep voice called just as the girls were in full spin. Sir Michael had trotted toward them and now sat atop his magnificent horse.

He bowed his head. "Lady Bonifay. Princess Aqua. I see that you are inspiring your realm again."

Princess Aqualine sighed. "I try but it seems that many scoff. Dost thou scoff too?"

Sir Michael hopped down from his steed and walked along beside the princess. "To me you will always be my lovely little Princess Aqua, tagging along behind your older brothers. But such memory is now a disservice. You are indeed an unusual young woman with ambitious ideas."

"Dost thou support Princess Aqualine?" Lady Bonifay asked.

"I honor thy efforts," he replied diplomatically.

"Tis not the same. But I know I hang low on the royal ladder you must climb," Princess Aqualine responded, with just a touch of disappointment in her voice. Support from a knight such as Sir Michael could be so helpful.

Sir Michael's laugh was a huge explosion of sound. "Tis not true Little Princess Aqua. Service to you brings me great joy. But now, I must away to the castle as your brothers and the Queen have summoned me."

The knight bowed again and remounted his horse.

"Tell them their loyal subjects are suffering. Tell them their subjects need protection from the cold rains," Princess Aqualine called as Sir Michael and his horse thundered away. She stuck out her tongue at his departing shape.

"You should be nicer to Sir Michael," Lady Bonifay suggested.

"Oh, I fear he neither understands me nor appreciates my proclamations," she said.

Bonifay frowned. "But he is a grand knight of the realm and could be a big help to you. In fact, he doth remind me of the mighty *Thor*—what with his red hair and great beard."

"Perhaps. But you must agree. Of my ideas he is skeptical," Princess Aqualine said. She gathered her skirts and hopped across a puddle.

Lady Bonifay chose to walk around it and hurried behind the Princess. "He is a wise man and he wonders from whence the ideas come. To him, as to us all they seem equal part genius and part wizardry."

Aqualine stopped abruptly and looked hard at her lady in waiting. "Do you Lady Bonifay, worry from whence they come?"

"No Princess. I have great faith in you. The little princess in your head delivers ideas that help, and often make me laugh. I do not worry. But I do wonder."

J. G. Matheny

Chapter Seven

Present day

Bonita squealed. "Oh, I almost forgot! I have to tell you something!"

She hopped up and down on the bed. I was still pondering Mike as a modern-day *Thor*.

"Okay," I said distractedly.

"No. Come over here. It's really incredible. You won't believe it."

I propelled my computer chair closer to the bed, pumping with my butt and legs. It couldn't be that incredible if she'd forgotten about it all day.

Bonita sputtered, "Sophia came up to me in gym class today!"

"Oh, Bonita. I'm sorry she's so mean to you. She really needs to learn to mind her own business."

"No! That's just it! She wasn't mean. She was almost nice. She waited until her pack had left for the locker room and I was putting the basketballs back in the rack."

"What did she say?" I was incredulous. Sophia approaching Bonita? Being nice?

"Well, she first said she was sorry about yesterday and that everyone shouldn't have laughed at me when I was trying to climb the rope. I was really cool and said it was okay. I said I thought Ritchie Harrell was far more amusing and that I laughed at him, too, just to show her I didn't feel singled out."

"That was good."

"Then she asked if I was Lady Bonita, your Lady in Waiting? She said that a few people she knew listened to our webcasts, and liked what we talked about."

Oh my gosh. This was *extreme.*

"And…" I prompted.

"I told her that we—that you—want to inspire and lead kids to be better citizens of our realm. That parents are well-meaning, but that kids can inspire each other better sometimes. And that's why you're *Princess Allison the Benevolent.* You give them guidance to make good decisions and act less selfishly. I didn't mention the part about your royal dreams and the Renaissance princess talking to you. I figured I'd skip that part."

"What did she say then?"

Bonita shrugged. "She asked how many kids listened."

I pointed to the computer screen proudly. "We had forty- eight tonight. It was a new record."

"I told Sophia we had about forty listening each night, but that our audience was bigger since not everyone can listen every night. So, I figure we have at least double that number, right? Do you know what she said to me?"

"No. What?"

"She said she thought we had more than that."

"How does she know?"

"She's been asking around. Princess Allison, she said she wants to meet with you tomorrow. She told me to tell you to look for her in the library after lunch."

J. G. Matheny

Chapter Eight

The Present

Bonita went home after helping me guess four or five reasons why Sophia wanted to meet with me. It really had me puzzled and just a bit worried. Sophia and I hadn't spoken since fifth grade.

I skipped lunch to read, so I found myself in the library half an hour before my scheduled meeting with Sophia. I thought if I were a loyal subject, what advice would I give myself? How should I act around someone who had once been a really close friend, and then grew up to be such a snob? Since I called myself The Benevolent, I was probably stuck with acting that way. But how was I going to pull that off?

It was because of Sophia's meanness that I'd started my webcasts to begin with. I wanted to help other kids deal with a Sophia in their lives, and I wanted to somehow influence them not to become like her.

I'd read a story about *Princess Aqualine the Wise* and how she issued daily proclamations that helped her kingdom. Back then life was so hard and people were so angry. Princess Aqualine led her loyal subjects into the Renaissance when music, art and happiness

41

flourished. She was just my age when she started her messages to her kingdom.

What if I did my own proclamations, I'd wondered? Dad had set up my computer, so my proclamations could be webcasts. Then the magic started and I began hearing Princess Aqualine in my dreams. I didn't worry about Sophia after that.

Until now, of course.

I perused a vintage hardcover *Harry Potter*. I figured that if Harry went to my school, he'd believe that I spoke with a Renaissance princess in my dreams. I'd just popped the book back onto the library shelf when Sophia peered around the corner. When she saw me, she stuck out her hip and swished her long silky hair in a trademark move. Then she tossed her purse over her shoulder and slumped into a round library chair.

She wore a jean skirt over beige leggings that stopped mid-calf, and a perfect light yellow cashmere short-sleeved sweater that showed off her *development*. Her toe nails were painted a perfect red. I could see this because she was wearing beaded flip flops. Who wears flip flops in Wisconsin during the spring rainy season?

"Where are your *Gators*?" I asked as an opener, sliding my butt onto the edge of the chair next to her. We had to sit closer than I'd prefer because, after all, we were in a library and expected to keep our voices down.

"Oh yeah. Oh well," she flipped her foot delicately, "these are prettier."

I shook my head. "Sometimes that's not the point," I said.

Sophia pouted. "No. Sometimes that's not *your* point. My point is always to be prettier."

"But don't you think there are other considerations? Like

comfort and whether you'll catch cold when it rains and you get your feet wet?" I asked.

Sophia squirmed a little.

"Those are considerations for you, Ally. You can wear jeans and that hoody you have on today because they make sense. I have to decide my clothes, and, well, everything else because they look pretty."

Sophia hadn't called me Ally in a long time. Not since we were best friends. Hearing it made my throat thick and my eyes sting.

I said, "Okay. What ever. It's just that on my webcasts this week I've suggested people wear *Gators* to keep their feet dry and not ruin their other shoes. I like your flip flops, but they'd get soaked walking to the bus and the leather would crinkle."

"My mom picks me up," Sophia said.

That's right. Normal kids take the bus. Sophia's mom picks her up in that big white SUV. This wasn't starting off well. It wasn't fair that she was making me squirm when she'd asked to see me in the first place.

"Okay. I just mentioned the webcast because Bonita told me you were asking questions…"

"Lady Bonita, right? That's what you call her? And you're *Princess Allison the Benevolent?*"

I couldn't tell if Sophia was making fun.

"It's not like we're cartoon characters, Sophia. My teachers don't call me princess. It's just who we are each night. And kids send us messages on our blog with their concerns and tune in to hear advice. And I, well, *Princess Allison*, tries hard to make it fair and helpful advice that encourages kids to be honest and good citizens," I said.

"Do you think I'm a good citizen?" Sophia asked.

"Actually, I spend some of my time counseling kids how to ignore people like you and take you less seriously. But that's usually one-on-one on the blog and not on the webcast. More personal, you know." I laughed.

Sophia smiled for the first time. "Thanks. I suppose it would be pretty obvious who you were talking about if you did it on the webcast. Do you ever have guests?"

I frowned. "It's really not an interview program. I suppose we could but we haven't before."

"But you could?"

"It would depend on what the guest would say. Do you want to be a guest, Sophia?"

Could that be what she wanted?

Sophia took a deep breath.

"Maybe. I need to reach a lot of people and I just don't know the best way to do it."

Oh my gosh! A thought popped into my head. Could she be this shallow?

"Sophia, you can't use my webcast to run for *Yearbook*! It's not that kind of forum! I can't believe you'd even think to ask me."

My voice was getting too loud for the library, but I wanted to let her *have* it. I stopped quickly, though. Her face had gone pale and she looked ready to cry.

"Oh no, Ally. That's not it. I can't blame you for thinking the worst of me, but really, I need it for a good cause. A really good cause. Nobody at school knows about it yet. We've been keeping it a secret at home but I heard my parents talking the other night and they're at the end of their rope and then I got the idea that maybe

Princess Allison the Benevolent could help."

Sophia was crying now. Softly because we were in the library. I let her whimper for a minute until it looked like she was under control. I slid my butt into the chair and scooted it up closer to hers. Sophia slumped forward when she was ready and whispered.

"My dad lost his job last year. We had to swear to keep it a secret. I thought everything was going okay until my mom and dad started fighting and I heard talk about losing the house and the cars."

Sophia lived in the golf course neighborhood where we used to live when my Mom and Dad were married. Her dad had some high-powered job as an investment banker and every year they got a new *Escalade* or *Lexus*.

Sophia continued, "Anyway, my brother couldn't try out for High School football this year because he might get injured and we don't have medical insurance any more. You know, because my dad lost his job? And for some reason...and I don't know why, Dad can't find another one."

Aha, I thought. Her brother Jason was so good at football in middle school. Rumors said that his grades weren't good enough to play in high school, so that's why he didn't play. But this made more sense.

"Well..." Sophia's voice started to squeak. "Jason needs an operation. Nobody's told me for sure what's wrong—but I know it's serious. First, I overheard my mom and dad talking and fighting about it. Then mom started acting strange and scared. At first, I just thought she was being cranky. Then she'd yell at us for no reason and then run upstairs to cry. I thought that was just because of having no money and being so worried. Mom and I used to go shopping a lot together and we'd spend lots of money on clothes and shoes. We haven't been able to do that anymore. I tried once. I took her credit card and went to the mall with Jennifer, but the store said the card wasn't any good. I had to put all the clothes back, and I really needed them."

The part about not getting the clothes caused real tears to fall on Sophia's cheeks, smearing her makeup. I didn't have a tissue or I would have given her one.

"About your mom?" I prompted, wanting to keep her on track.

"I heard her on the phone yesterday. I think she was talking to the doctor's office. Jason had some tests done. Anyway, she kept telling the doctor's office, no, there's no money. Then she hung up and lay down on the kitchen floor in a ball and just cried and cried and cried. It was so awful."

Oh my gosh.

"Can't they borrow some money? Like from a bank?" I asked.

Sophia shook her head. The blond mane swished around.

"My dad can't get any money from the bank because he owes so much already."

"How about from friends or your grandparents?"

"Oh no! That's the worst part. This is all a secret. We can't tell anybody anything! My dad would go crazy if he knew I was telling you. He says the money problems are a family matter and we'll handle it ourselves. So, we can't borrow any money from people because then the neighbors would know my dad lost his job and we weren't being the way we're supposed to be."

"Well, what is that, exactly? The way you're supposed to be?"

Sophia kind of gasped. "We're supposed to be rich and fabulous."

"Okay. So, who really cares if you're not?"

"Oh Ally…Don't you know? Really?"

I shook my head, no. I didn't know. Really.

"*Everybody* cares. If people knew my dad was broke and couldn't get a job, and if we lost our house and our cars, do you think I'd still be the coolest girl in the school like I am now? Do you think people would still want to be friends with me?"

I thought Sophia was going to choke on that last sentence. She looked so sad slumped in the library chair.

J. G. Matheny

Chapter Nine
The Renaissance

My loyal subjects, Princess Aqualine welcomes you to today's declaration. My idea from earlier this week has me so excited! Such passion doth engulf me! Our kingdom's alchemists labor now to make my Gators and concoct enough of the resin to keep our coats and roofs and houses warm and dry. One noble alchemist hath proclaimed that this rubber first comes from a plant that grows afar. Our mixologists must work their magic to fashion into footwear or spread upon our roofs. Won't that be amazing? Think thee of all the sickness and disease to never again plague our people. Think thee that rather dry and warm be our fate? The wee babes of our kingdom with no coughs that last for days and weeks wracking their little bodies until weak and feverish? I say this concoction may be our gift to make our world better.

Aqualine stopped, her quill poised above the page.

"Lady Bonifay, dost thou think I am daft pledging loyal subjects' time to create my brightly colored footwear?"

Today Lady Bonifay thought pink ribbons would look best in Princess Aqualine's hair. The rain had stopped after yesterday and the skies were clear. It smelled like springtime. And she found pink so lively a color. Lady Bonifay would never attempt the color herself. Her skin was too pale. Red was a better hue for her but alas it did not scream of spring as much as pink. Or yellow. Perhaps blue? That might work, she mused.

The princess' question roused her. "Milady, I am your most loyal servant..."

"I know thou art, but would thou tell me true what you think?" Princess Aqualine persisted.

Lady Bonifay laid the ribbons carefully side by side on the dressing table. She pursed her lips and took her time forming the right words.

"Lady Saraphina has taken to calling you *Princess Aqualine the Silly* instead of *Princess Aqualine the Wise*."

Princess Aqualine watched her with a solemn look. "Oh, tis hard to lead with an idea such as this in my head," she bemoaned. "I know 'tis truly *out there*... (*Ugh*, yet more baffling words in my head and from my dreams). But I believe in my heart that we will transform our lives!"

Lady Bonifay nodded. "If you will grant my open tongue?"

"By all means, speak!" Aqualine commanded.

Lady Bonifay hung her head.

"My Princess, I embraced your *Snuggly* vision when it came onto you, and I even cut the first patterns from canvas cloth before we learned to craft them from warmer and cozier weavings. And my father met with such trials constructing your top of the lap desk. It was uncomfortable on the knees, and it slid so quickly off your skirts."

Princess Aqualine nodded. "Ah, but these were helpful ideas.

And 'tis *lap top desk*."

"But this idea, milady? It is very big and many are now counting upon its success. Pray if your *Stretchy* amazes as the *Snuggly*, then so many lives will be transformed. Feet will be dry," Lady Bonifay said.

"Dost thou worry that it might fail?"

Bonifay nodded reluctantly. "I know that my dear father has mixed his own concoction. He has found passion, but has started two fires thus far in our meager house trying to heat the material hot enough to stretch and wrap around a shoe."

"But he is a baker!" Princess Aqualine cried.

"Who better to work with chemistry?" Lady Bonifay replied.

"But Lady Saraphina and her *pack* have been cruel," Princess Aqualine said.

"Yes, Milady. She called you a *child*. She said you are playing with dolls and diverting our realm's alchemists from real problems to make *doll shoes*." Lady Bonifay picked up the two pink ribbons to weave through Princess Aqualine's hair.

"Dost she have followers?" Aqualine asked.

Lady Bonifay frowned. "Ah but yes. Some."

J. G. Matheny

Chapter Ten

The Present

Good evening loyal subjects. Princess Allison the Benevolent here, checking in for my nightly webcast. We've made it through the soggy week and I promise this weekend will be more fun. Make a list of those things you would like to do outdoors, and I challenge you all to pledge to do them before the weekend is over. I know that I am not alone in recalling sitting in front of the window, watching the perpetual rain and saying to myself, "If only it was sunny. I would be riding my bike." Or, "If only the rain would stop, I would run next door and see what those kids were doing."

Well, the time is now. The rain has stopped. So, let's put down the phones, roll off that couch and find our strong legs. Vow to run out the front door—letting it slam if it must—and catapult yourself to the seat of your trusty bike and ride out to explore!

Imagine that you were living in the year 1590 and there were no bikes. Only rain and disease and work. Celebrate the fact that you don't live then, and that you live now!

Before I sign off tonight, I want to talk about setting priorities. I know you've heard this from your parents before, but it makes sense. If our priorities are in order, then everything is fine. But if our priorities get out of order, then everything can get messed up. I met this week with a loyal subject whose family priorities are severely out of whack.

For those of you listening, I think that we can help our fellow loyal subject fix her priorities. Send Princess Allison the Benevolent a message on our blog right now. Think very carefully and tell us the things that are most important to you in your lives. Be wise and thoughtful. I know many of you value your I Pods and Smartphones. That's not what we're looking for here. Extra Benevolent points will be awarded to the loyal subject truly understanding this assignment and delivering to me some good ideas. Princess Allison the Benevolent signing off.

"If you'll pardon the affront, Princess Allison, but that last part didn't make much sense. You had me confused, and when I'm confused, our loyal subjects generally are too. The responses are going to suck. Why can't you just tell me what this is all about? Maybe I could help," Bonita said.

She sat at the corner of my bed. A big drop of peanut butter hung from the celery stick she held in her left hand, dangerously close to dropping on my yellow fur pillow in her lap. In the nick of time, Bonita's tongue stretched out and lapped it up.

"Mmm," she sighed. Bonita was so happy when she was fed.

"I can't tell you just yet."

"Does this have something to do with you and Sophia meeting

today? You've been acting really strange ever since."

Lying to Bonita wasn't something I liked doing. Before I said the first thing that jumped into my head, which was of course a lie, I thought for a moment just of whom I owed an allegiance. Sophia had told me a big secret. But her reasoning was that I could help her out.

So she was actually using me.

Don't get me wrong. I was happy that she wanted help and that she came to me. Or actually, she came to *Princess Allison the Benevolent*. I'm not getting a big head here, I promise.

Bonita, on the other hand, trusts me unquestioningly.

She never betrayed any confidence. Okay, I was worried that if I told her, she might secretly be happy with Sophia's misfortune, but I suppose that would be human.

Sophia was such a snob. She'd ended our friendship when my dad left, and mom and I had to move from the big house to this townhouse. We didn't mind that we had to do this. After all, it was a good solution to our money problems and it helped my mom a lot. She didn't have to see happy families everyday and be reminded that hers wasn't anymore.

But for some reason, this change in our status had mattered to Sophia and we couldn't be friends anymore.

I think Sophia was upset that my family fell apart and disrupted her world. Like, I wasn't around anymore to play with. My mom wasn't around anymore to give rides and makes cookies. Sophia's mom never baked. She just worked out at the health club. My dad wasn't around to play basketball in the driveway on late summer evenings. Most dads shot hoops with their sons. Mine was special because he played with us girls. Sophia learned her jump shot from my dad.

"Okay Bonita. I was going to tell you just as soon as I figure out what to do."

Bonita's eyes bulged. She smashed the celery stick into the peanut butter, standing it up on itself.

"It is about Sophia, isn't it? Did she make fun of *Princess Allison*? Something inside of me said she was setting you up."

"No, she didn't make fun. I thought she might, too. I couldn't figure it out. I thought and thought. I could have fallen on my butt with surprise when I found out. She needs our *help*. I mean, she needs *Princess Allison's* help."

"Oh my gosh. What for?"

I considered just one moment more, weighing whether to tell, and then the words, just like a volcano's lava, erupted from my mouth.

"Her brother needs an operation. Her dad's out of a job and they can't afford to pay for it because the operation is too expensive. Her mom cries all the time because she is so worried. They're not allowed to tell anybody about their money problems. It's this big family secret. But Sophia thinks that if her brother doesn't get the operation, he'll never play sports again. And her mom and dad will stay so worried and upset that they'll break up. And then, basically, she'd turn out like me. Personally, I think that's what scares her the most."

Bonita jumped up in surprise.

"That's crazy. They have that big house and those really cool cars. And Sophia's clothes…"

I gulped. "She's been going to *Goodwill* and shopping *EBAY*. She sells the clothes she grows out of and buys replacement ones for her and her mom. They haven't had any money for a really long time."

"But her pack? They're all really rich. They'd figure it out, you'd think?" Bonita advised.

I nodded. "Yes. She knew she was going to be discovered eventually. After all, the good stuff at *Goodwill* gets picked over really quick. Even if you are a good shopper."

Bonita stopped and looked at me. Her brow furrowed and she poked her under lip out.

"So, you feel sorry for Sophia?"

I thought for a moment.

"Yeah, I guess I do."

Bonita's lip started to quiver. I couldn't tell if she was angry or ready to cry.

"You can't feel sorry for her!" Bonita shouted. "She's just getting what's coming to her. So what if her pack learns she's broke and they kick her out? She's mean and she's selfish. All those things Princess Allison teaches her loyal subjects *not* to be. Sophia never needed you until there was something you could do for her!"

I swirled in my computer chair. I'd never seen Bonita so upset. She looked so hurt.

"Oh, no!" I cried. "That's not it, Bonita. Really."

J. G. Matheny

Chapter 11

The Renaissance

Princess Aqualine's pink ribbons sailed in the morning breeze. Every now and then the end of one caught in her mouth and she'd have to stop mid stride and push it away She could admit, the ribbons were too frivolous for the intensity of this morning. But, no, Aqualine wouldn't remove them. Plaiting them through her hair had pleased Lady Bonifay and now was not the time to alienate a loyal subject and good friend.

This morning's proclamation was posted only ten minutes before shouts erupted from townspeople gathered in the square. Was this truly out of hand, she wondered? Even calling the new substance a funny name such as *Stretchy* hadn't diminished the zeal. And was that another fist fight breaking out? Princess Aqualine ducked into St. Timothy's vestibule to watch.

"Little Princess Aqua, are you here for your prayers?"

The massive voice startled her and she jumped back from the door. At her side stood Sir Michael, bedecked in a lush brown tunic with gold braiding. His red hair and beard set his head ablaze.

"O me!" she cried.

"Did I frighten you, Little Princess?"

"Yes, brave knight, you did. But alas, not so much as our

townsfolk outside. I fear I have erred."

Sir Michael leaned against the heavy door and swung it closed. He guided her to a pew in the ancient church that was all quiet and empty now.

"Oh, Brave Princess, you take upon your shoulders such wise and reaching endeavors. But your youth prevents the guidance your loyal subjects need right now to please them," Sir Michael said.

Aqualine gazed at the knight. She watched his lips move under his red fuzzy mustache. His beard bobbed and he rested a giant hand on her shoulder. He'd frightened me so when I was little, she recalled, but this man today was surprisingly gentle. Princess Aqualine realized she really needed his help.

"What dost thou suggest?"

"You have ignited the imaginations of the realm and that is indeed laudable. Yet the virtuous move amidst rascals and wayfarers and your challenge to create *Stretchy*...pardon my efforts with this odd name."

Princess Aqualine winced. "I labor to find it's betterment but so far we have dubbed it *Stretchy*."

"You desire to create this odd substance, but it has had consequences that you did not foresee. Confusion and such fist fighting as now. Yet, say, I have an idea." He smiled. "Yay, a grand idea, indeed. We will hold a festival and judge our alchemists' concoctions. You will see, my little Princess Aqua, that with your wisdom and my might, together we will serve and protect the realm."

Princess Aqualine leaned in closer and listened to his idea, feeling better than she had in days.

Chapter 12

The Present

I wanted to hug Bonita and calm her down. She'd turned her back on me and was facing the wall with her arms folded defiantly. She was huffing and crying, and huffing and crying. I jumped up and stood behind her. I didn't want to invade her space, but I wanted her to know that I cared enough to be close.

"Why are you so upset?" I asked.

Bonita's body heaved again and she sucked in her breath.

"I don't know. Exactly. I'm trying to figure that out," she said in between sobs.

"Princess Allison helps kids, Bonita. Sometimes things upset me, too, but I have to stop and think, and try to put my own silly concerns aside to be the voice of *Princess Allison the Benevolent*. In this case, I think being benevolent means to be compassionate. Sophia has been mean and selfish. I agree. But she's in a bad situation now. You can't blame her for being so status conscious. Look at her parents! They want to pretend to the world that they're still better than everybody else, when in fact they have problems just like normal people. And they force their kids to keep their secret and not ask for any help. If Sophia's parents made family their priority instead of status, Sophia would be getting guidance and strength from *them*."

Bonita turned her face to me and wiped at her eyes. "So since her parents are messing up their priorities, Sophia needs to find this guidance and strength somewhere else. And so she came to you."

"She came to *Princess Allison the Benevolent* and her main Lady in Waiting. She came to us."

Bonita turned and I hugged her round body. The celery stick was still standing upright in the peanut butter. Bonita lifted the jar from the dresser and sat back on the corner of my bed to eat and calm down. I sat back in my computer chair and checked the blog for royal subject responses. Then I pulled out a pad to make a list of ways Princess Allison could help Sophia.

"Bonita, what do you think Sophia would be like if she wasn't, well...Sophia?"

"You mean if she was more like a normal kid?"

"Yeah."

Bonita giggled. "Well, honestly, I'd like to say that nobody would like her and she wouldn't have any friends, but Princess Allison the Benevolent would object to that kind of wishful thinking."

"Ummm. Princess Allison would say you were being envious and selfish."

"Okay. So I think Sophia is really pretty. She'd still be popular because she is so pretty. She'd probably have to work harder at it, though. No money for highlights and pedicures and clothes. She'd need to be friendlier, too, since fans just won't drop into her lap like before. Maybe she would be sporty instead of stuck up," Bonita replied.

I considered this. "Sophia is good at basketball and volleyball."

"Ugh. She'd have to change her attitude, though. The last time we played volleyball in gym, Sophia and her pack wouldn't touch the ball because it might break a fingernail. I'd work really hard to bump it up to one of them, and they'd let it go *plop*, right in front of the net. Not even try to get it." Bonita crossed her eyes, further illustrating her disgust with their lack of effort.

"She would have to try harder," I agreed.

"So, what exactly did she want Princess Allison to do to help her out?"

"To begin with, she wanted to appear with me on the webcast, and just ask kids to contribute to a really good cause."

"Oh my gosh. That would make her look like *Saint* Sophia, looking out for the underprivileged. She wasn't going to tell them, I presume, that *she* was the good cause?"

I laughed.

"I told her that we don't usually have guests, and it would be easier to protect her privacy if Princess Allison handled it alone."

"That was diplomatic. Why does she need privacy?"

"Her priorities are still messed up. She wants to help Jason get money for his surgery without letting anyone know about the family's money situation. Sophia wants to keep the secret."

"She won't be able to," Bonita said, wisely. "Word will get out."

Bonita was so right.

I said, "I think maybe we have to ease her into doing the right thing. To show her that everything won't collapse if the secret gets out. That kids can be trusted to understand and help."

"So that's why you had our loyal subjects send in their list of priorities!"

I nodded.

"Yup. I'm thinking we'll show her some of the responses and maybe she can talk to her mom and dad and convince them people really don't care about status. That kids care about more important things."

Bonita crossed her eyes at me and flopped back onto the bed.

"If you'll pardon the affront once more, Princess Allison, I really don't think that's the help Sophia is looking for. You'd be making her do something she's obviously afraid to do, and that's talking honestly with her mom and dad. And they still won't have enough money. "

Gosh, Bonita could really hit the target sometimes.

I said, "Well, okay. It was just my first idea. My brain is a little plugged up. Let's look at our loyal subject's responses. Maybe they'll surprise us."

I twisted back around to the computer and clicked my mouse on the blog message board. The printer whirred and Bonita aroused herself from my puffy fur pillow, crossed to the edge of the computer desk where my printer was perched, and studied the first page. She scrunched her nose.

"I think they missed your point, Princess Allison. One thinks the world would be a better place if skateboarding was our Number One priority. Another believes dogs rank higher than parents. That weird guy who calls himself Nerd2Beat sent us half a page of math calculations."

"What do you suppose he means by that?"

Bonita giggled. "Dunno. Maybe happiness equals math? We get some strange stuff sometimes."

"It's just harder for Princess Allison to help Sophia with her priorities when it looks like our loyal subjects haven't a clue about theirs either."

Bonita rested her butt on my lap and stared at the computer screen. Then she stood up and headed for the peanut butter jar.

Between mouthfuls of peanut butter coated celery, she said, "You know, Princess Allison, it really doesn't matter what our loyal subjects have to say. You're the one we all listen to. You're the one who counsels us. So maybe it will be up to only *you* to fix Sophia. And if you haven't any ideas, then maybe you'll have to ask for help."

J. G. Matheny

Chapter 13

The Renaissance

My loyal subjects of the kingdom of LaPoste, welcome to today's proclamation. It seems that ever since I raised the discussion into that magic substance I reluctantly dub Stretchy, my subjects have clamored for more details on its development. Many of you have realized that the development of Stretchy could mean riches for whomever discovers it. I personally think the true riches will come to whomever fashions my Gators, but I suppose my opinion doesn't really count in this exciting time of invention.

I am disappointed to report that the potential for riches has tainted this scientific odyssey. After I was witness to a fist fight in the town square as one noble alchemist attempted to convince another that his concoction was superior, I sought the aide of our kingdom's bravest knight, Sir Michael the Moral. He has recommended a remarkable solution!

We will hold a festival in one week's time and a contest in the town square. Every alchemist who wishes to participate must bring a sample of their Stretchy. And if that alchemist should want to seek my approval, he should also bring a model for my Gators. The entries will be judged and he who has developed the best product will be awarded the credit for this revolutionary discovery, and a place in history.

I want to thank Sir Michael the Moral for this glowing solution. My mother, the Queen, will be the honorary host for this judging contest. Our kingdom's chief wizard will be the head judge. It will be a memorable and historic event.

Princess Aqualine the Wise wishes you a good evening.

"Your proclamation impresses, dear princess," Lady Bonifay said as she brushed Aqualine's hair. "I was wrong about your idea. It seems to be a wise and timely invention. The women in the kingdom are terribly excited about how it can improve a child's chance for survival. So many of the little tykes get ill during the winter, from the snow and the wet and cold inside their homes. *Stretchy* can weatherproof their homes and keep illness away."

"Oh, thank you! I am so happy to have your support. This is truly the most exciting time!"

Lady Bonifay surveyed her masterful job with Aqualine's hair in the mirror.

"And you seem to be patching things up with Sir Michael. I told you he could be counted upon to be kind and helpful."

Aqualine sighed and handed her scroll to Lady Bonifay.

"I didn't want to work with him, you know. I was once so afraid of his monstrous size and huge voice. It would make me run away and hide as a child. But I have seen what a good friend he has been to my brothers and the Queen. He is like Thor. He is much more than a marvel."

"If you will pardon my correction, Princess Aqualine, but a marvel is a marvel. It is absolute. There is not *more than a marvel*."

Aqualine laughed. "I see your point. Anyway, he is still highly skeptical of how I developed my rubber, or *Stretchy* idea that started all this craziness!"

Bonifay nodded solemnly. "He doesn't believe that you have a princess from the future inside your head?"

"Aha? Who would believe such a thing? But she has made me *Princess Aqualine the Wise*."

Lady Bonifay handed her a dressing gown.

"Yes, and shortly to be known as the brilliant inspiration behind the development of *Stretchy*!"

J. G. Matheny

Chapter 14

Present day

"Allison! Bonita's mom wants her home. Come down for dinner!"

Ughh.

"Time to go, Lady Bonita. We'll work on this tomorrow," I said, gathering up the printed responses from the loyal subjects, and stuffing them where they belonged—into my waste basket.

"How should I act tomorrow in gym?" Bonita asked as she skipped down my stairs. I think she was delighting just a little in Sophia's fall from perfection.

"Like regular. But I'd be prepared for Sophia to act a little stranger to you than usual."

"Do you think she might actually talk to me again?" Bonita seemed excited by the possibility.

I shrugged as I opened our front door. It was refreshing to see the porch dry and the driveway no longer muddy. It smelled like a mix of spring time and my mom's lasagna. My mouth started to water. Bonita's peanut butter hadn't been that appealing, but mom's lasagna? That was another story.

I said, "Yeah, she might. But just in case, don't get your feelings hurt if she doesn't. Sophia doesn't want people to know she has a problem, remember? She might even be meaner."

Bonita stopped. "Over-compensating, right?"

"Yes, that's what they call it. Just remind yourself she's come to us for help, and we're going to help her."

I closed the door behind Bonita, hoping for the best.

As I rounded the hallway into our kitchen, I stopped cold. Mom hadn't said anything about Mike being here. I hadn't seen Bigfoot since the other night. But there he was, sitting in the white captain's chair at the head of our country cabin wood table, his enormous legs bulging forth beneath the wooden top. My mother sat next to him, dishing the lasagna onto plates with a spatula. They both looked up and caught me staring.

"Hi, Honey. Mike has a stake-out tonight, so I thought it would be nice that he stop by for dinner first."

Mike smiled and white teeth emerged out from under his huge mash of lips and red beard. He actually looked kind of cute. He lifted a clinched fist pump.

"Kids rule!" he huffed, and then shoveled a forkful of pasta and cheese into his mouth. Swallowing after only three chews, he planted a wet kiss on my mom's cheek.

"Just fabulous," he said. Then to me, "Come and sit with us, Princess. Tell us what's going on in your world. "

Whoa...no way! Who does this guy think he is? Part of the family?

I was ready to blurt something distracting and run back upstairs when I thought about two things. The first was that I hadn't yet thanked him for my pink scarf and furry journal. I needed to be polite. Princess Allison would be very critical of any behavior that wasn't at the very least, polite.

My *second* thought was that I was amazingly hungry.

Mike winked at me.

"Come on. Sit. Eat. You think too much for a kid."

I shrugged and obediently slid into the chair opposite Mom. She had a goofy expression on her face when she looked at Mike. It was silky and smiley and happy. She cut a large square from the pan and placed the lasagna on my plate. She heaped a couple stalks of asparagus close by.

Mike chomped on his asparagus and watched me. When I finally looked up into his face, he winked again.

"You usually this quiet?"

Mom's words gushed out before I could say a word. "Oh, she's just a little tired from school and her nightly webcast. How'd it go tonight, honey?"

They both watched me like I was a baby, about to spit up. Waiting for words to upchuck onto the table.

"It was okay," I said. Then I dove into my lasagna. Thankfully they respected my feeding frenzy and laid off the questions for a minute. They still stared, though.

I swallowed.

"So, who are you staking out?" I asked, diverting attention from me.

"We've got a couple guys planning a bank robbery. Caught them on video a couple weeks back robbing the Third Savings Bank downtown. We got a tip saying they're planning to take down another bank tomorrow morning. We want to catch them in the act."

Wow.

I asked, "What would they do to you if they found out you're there, watching?"

Mike laughed.

"Well, Princess, we're pretty good. We don't plan to be caught. We plan to catch *them*. But, in answer to your question, they probably would just call off their plans. Lay low. Pretend they were planning a trip to the beach and not a bank heist. There wouldn't be a shoot out like you see in the movies, if that's what you're wondering."

I nodded. That was exactly what I was wondering. If police work was as dangerous as we kids see on TV, I figure there wouldn't be many police around. They'd either be dead, or their kids would have convinced them to take a job as an accountant or *Wal-Mart* store manager, or something else less risky.

An idea for a Princess Allison webcast was formulating. *Meet the Real Police. The Police are our friend.*

Pretty lame titles. What had Bonita said the other day? That Mike reminded her of *Thor*. But not all police looked like Mike, so a program called *Police—The Modern-Day Thor* wouldn't be good.

Maybe a knight in shining armor? That was it! Where had that idea come from? *Our Modern-day Knights*. Now, that was a good title.

Mike's big foot kicked my leg.

"You're thinkin' too much again, Princess…"

Okay. Bonita was right. Princess Allison needed help.

"I've got a, well, let's just call her a *friend*, who's in trouble. Her family is out of money and her brother needs an operation and they don't have insurance. She's come to me. Well, she's come to *Princess Allison the Benevolent* for help. And I'm not sure what to do for her."

To my surprise, Mom pried herself from Mike's side and came

over, sat down next to me and gave me a big, long hug.

"Oh, honey. I'm so sorry for your friend. I figured there might come a time when you'd be asked to solve something tougher than footwear issues."

"Mom, the *Gators* segment was very popular," I blurted, defensively.

But I knew what she meant.

I said, "*Princess Allison the Benevolent* only exists in the web world. She hasn't had to really do something before."

Mom interrupted. "I disagree. She's helped kids make the right decisions and do the right thing. Those are really big things."

I guess I hadn't realized she understood.

Mike chomped an asparagus spear thoughtfully.

"I have an idea," he said. "Let's put on a fund raiser for the sick kid. My department does it all the time. We can hold it at the fairgrounds. We can charge an admission, have games and rides... sell food and baked goods that folks have donated. Even have a raffle. All the money goes to pay for the operation. The whole police force shows up. Radio stations promote it and the community comes out. It's great."

Mike winked at mom and me. "Stop thinkin' so hard, Princess. Problem solved."

J. G. Matheny

Chapter 15

Present day

My loyal subjects, Princess Allison the Benevolent here to tell you about a great event happening this weekend at the LaPoste fairgrounds. It's a fund raiser for one of our realm who is in dire need of an operation. Now, as you can imagine, his family doesn't want everyone to know that they're broke and can't afford this operation, so we're keeping his name a secret. But trust your Royal Princess that your support and participation in this fund-raising fair is very important. So, tell your friends and bring your family. It will be great fun and every penny is going to this very worthy cause.

Princess Allison herself is going to be very busy for the next couple days coordinating this event with my new friends at the LaPoste police department. These police are such wonderful protectors of our community. If we were all living five hundred years ago, these guardians would be known as the Knights of our Kingdom. Come out Saturday and pay them homage, and eat some turkey legs and cake. My Queen mother is making her famous lasagna. Trust me, that it is a mouth-watering treat!

See you all there!

Princess Allison the Benevolent signing off.

Bonita slid from my bed. She said, "I'm hungry. You're talking too much about lasagna. This is going to be a great event, Princess Allison. I'm proud to help, and once again, to be your Lady in Waiting."

I gulped and gave Bonita a hug.

She continued. "And you seem to be patching things up with Mike. He's working really hard on this fair."

"You're right. I'm starting to call him Sir Michael."

"Really? Is that another character from the Renaissance princess in your head?"

"Uh-huh. Sir Michael the Moral was a huge knight who helped *Princess Aqualine the Wise* accomplish her great deeds. They were a great team, but they didn't get along well at first either."

Chapter 16

The Renaissance

Dear loyal subjects of the kingdom of LaPoste, Princess Aqualine the Wise is issuing her proclamation on the eve of our great festival. As you must all know by now, Sir Michael the Moral had suggested this fair to recognize our alchemists' efforts in the development of rubber, or Stretchy as Lady Bonifay dubs it, and the creation of my Princess footwear known as Gators. History will credit the winner of tomorrow's judging with these amazing contributions to society. With dry feet and dry houses, my loyal subjects will live longer and prosper.

Come one! Come all to the town square festival tomorrow. I have been coordinating closely with Sir Michael and his fellow brave knights of our kingdom to ensure that tomorrow's event is both successful and fun. Tell your friends and bring your families. Princess Aqualine the Wise wishing you a fond good day.

"Come walk with me now, Lady Bonifay. Let us post this and see the excitement in the market."

They walked carefully down the winding castle steps and into the courtyard. Carts rolled by carrying loyal subjects on their way to the marketplace or back home to plant crops or feed their animals. Princess Aqualine waved her hand to as many as possible.

A rough looking man kicked his foot into the hair.

"Yay, Princess! I can't wait for our *Stretchy* boots. These are all leaky."

Aqualine could see the sole flapping away from the leather boot.

She laughed. "My goodness! I don't believe we'll have anything developed in time to replace those! You'll need to find a cobbler, sir."

Lady Bonifay frowned. "Oh no, Lady Saraphina is coming."

Princess Aqualine sighed. "Lady Bonifay, both you and I worry that the Princess in my head has conceived something too large for our realm. That has allowed our loyal subjects expectations to soar, perchance to crash. Saraphina speaks our greatest fear. We must meet her with graciousness."

Lady Saraphina's hair escaped her usually perfect braid, and an apron was tied to her waist.

"Princess Aqualine, I am happy to find you. Have you another proclamation?"

Lady Bonifay stuck out her chin. "For you to scoff?"

"Oh no, have I ever scoffed?" Saraphina smiled. "My father has dispatched me to find you herewith. He believes that he has concocted your *Stretchy*. I have not seen him so full of life for many years. He has been so sad. Our fortunes changed and he was required to farm but he is not happy as a farmer. He is a mixologist. My mother sang your praises just this morning with special thanks for electrifying his spirit and perhaps doing great good for the land. When I told her of what great friends we were, she sent me straight away to confirm the arrangements for the fair."

Lady Bonifay looked shocked. "Saraphina, I do not recall your friendship."

Saraphina's head dropped. "Perhaps I have teased too much. But this idea, this competition, has changed my family for the better."

"Lady Bonifay, let us embrace our loyal subject as we have met a need in her family, as well as one within our realm," Princess Aqualine said, stepping forward and putting her arms around Saraphina. "I will speak with Sir Michael and insure your father a prominent position, up front where he can dazzle the judges."

Lady Bonifay was not so easily impressed by Saraphina's contrition. "Do your fellow ladies..."

"My pack?"

"Well, yes. Do they know of your father's interest in the competition? In Princess Aqualine's idea?"

Saraphina hesitated. "They know some. And of what they know, they have their reservations. But I see joy once again in my father's countenance. To my mother, 'tis like the heavens opening. I know Father will win."

Princess Aqualine unrolled the parchment, and together with Saraphina and Lady Bonifay, they attached it to the center post at the town square.

"Our best wishes for luck to you and your father!" Princess Aqualine called as Saraphina ran home. From close by, she heard a great whinny, and Sir Michael charged into the square on his enormous horse.

He laughed as Lady Bonifay stepped in front of the princess, and stretched out her arms as a shield.

"Dost he frighten you?"

Lady Bonifay gulped and lowered her arms. Princess Aqualine stepped forward.

"It is her reflex to protect me. Your horse, and you, did frighten me at one time. When I was a little girl. But no longer."

Lady Bonifay bowed. "We see you as our modern-day Thor. A defender of our realm."

Sir Michael smiled grandly through his mustache and beard.

"Thor. I like that. Worry not about tomorrow's festivities. Your realm will respond. We will have our winner *and* we will have a remarkable invention."

Sir Michael laughed as he rode away. It was a thunderous roar, his red head and beard shaking with the effort.

Chapter 17
Present Day

Bonita presented me with a massive grilled turkey leg. The drumstick bone was as thick as my wrist.

"My mom and I cooked them to perfection. "

"These are *yours*?" I cried in disbelief. A kid with a balloon ran past and almost tripped Bonita as she spun around proudly.

"My mom and I cooked up four platters of turkey drumsticks for today's fair. I convinced her that every kid needed good quality protein in their diet. Even kids like me with a few extra pounds. She listened to our food pyramid webcast and *Princess Allison the Benevolent* advice. Then she consulted with my pediatrician."

"Instead of her personal trainer?"

"Exactly. An expert on children's nutritional issues. And, voila! We shopped together, and I helped her cook."

"Why didn't you tell me earlier?" I asked.

Bonita stuck her lower lip out in thought, and then smiled.

"You've been really busy with Mike and his police buddies, setting things up for the fair. Besides I wanted to surprise you! You and Mike are getting along really well now, right?"

This time I stuck my lower lip out in thought.

"He's really great," I said finally.

"But he still doesn't get this *Princess Allison* thing yet, right?"

I shrugged.

"He's catching on."

Bonita squealed in laughter.

"You liar! No, he's not! He got you that shirt you're wearing today! I just know it!"

I moved my turkey leg in front of my body to cover up the sparkly lettering on my pink tank top. It read, *I'm A Princess.*

"Nah, he just wanted all my loyal subjects to be able to recognize me."

"Yeah, right!" Bonita laughed. "Did you ever thank him for the fuzzy journal and the pink scarf?"

I pulled the scarf from my hip pocket.

"Yup. I'm using the scarf as a bandana. And Mom has the journal up at the reception table, taking everyone's name as they come in. Let's go see how she's doing."

Bonita and I maneuvered past a circle of five-year-olds grouped around a clown in a Police Uniform reading a funny story. The kids were squealing and poking each other. One kept bouncing up to the clown and pulling at his huge red nose.

We walked through the monstrous white circus tent where tables and chairs were set in the middle of endless tables of food and bakery treats. Police officers in jeans and t-shirts bearing the LaPoste Police Department (LPD) insignia served up the plates to moms and dads and kids streaming through the line. It was noisy and smelled of BBQ ribs, lasagna and coffee. I grabbed a cup of coffee and a homemade Blondie for mom, but the police officer refused to let me drop a couple dollars in the donation can.

"No way, Princess. You made this all happen. Your stuff is free today," he said.

I smiled. How cool.

The reception table was located under a huge rainbow arc of balloons at the entry to the fairground. A line of maybe twenty people stood quietly to pay their admission and join the hundreds already inside.

I carefully placed the coffee next to mom's cash box, and the Blondie beside and gave her a quick kiss on the cheek. Her skin smelled like Chanel NO. 5 and sunscreen. She smiled and chatted with the lady paying in front of her.

"No, we don't know the name of the boy who will get the operation. His family wants to keep it all a secret, so we're respecting their wishes. My boyfriend Mike is on the Police force. He's going to have the check presented to the family through my daughter here, whose been coordinating it all." Mom looked at me and smiled proudly.

"So, you must be *Princess Allison the Benevolent,*" the lady in line said to me. "My son listens to your program every night. He convinced me to get a better computer set-up so that he could. He follows your rules. He's very well behaved now and much more considerate of his younger brother. We still have trouble with him writing math equations all over the place, but I figure he'll grow up to be another *Einstein.*"

Bonita yanked my arm and rolled her eyes. Our weird loyal subject *Nerd2Beat* had a mother!

I heard a rustling in line. Coming towards us were Jennifer and Haley from Sophia's pack. Each wore a cute, short denim skirt with cream leggings and Ugh boots. Neither one smiled; as if attending the fair was the most un-cool thing they'd ever been asked to do.

They separated at the reception table, plunked their five-dollar bills in front of my mom, and looked past Bonita and I with a couple tosses of their heads and sniffs.

Then Sophia emerged from behind them.

She walked up to the table. Her head started to twitch like she was going to swish her magnificent blonde hair in the signature Sophia move. But she stopped mid-motion.

"Hello, Mrs. Warner. It's good to see you again," she said to my mom politely.

"Well, hello Sophia. I'm happy to see you coming out for a good cause. It's been a long time. How are your mom and dad? Your brother?"

Bonita and I grunted at the same time. Mom didn't notice, but Sophia looked up.

"They're okay, I guess. Ooohh, here's Allison. I need to say hi to her."

"You *do*?" Mom asked.

Mom didn't miss much, including the last couple years I'd been frozen out of Sophia's life. Sophia dropped her five dollars in Mom's palm and turned to walk toward us.

Mom's voice trailed behind her, "Say hi to your mother for me. She and I were friends when we lived in the old neighborhood."

"I remember," Sophia called over her shoulder.

Bonita, Sophia and I walked slowly away from the reception table. We were an awkward assortment of pre-teenagers: Sophia in her black mini skirt and vintage tank top that, I figured she'd bought off E-Bay. Bonita in her oversized white t-shirt and cammo pants, and me in my pink princess top and jeans. We reached a shade tree that offered some privacy from the exuberantly successful fair.

Sophia looked around. Then she started to cry.

"I can't believe this. All these people coming out. My brother's going to be okay now. I just know it."

Sophia whimpered a little more. Bonita passed her a napkin she'd used for the turkey leg and Sophia blew her nose.

"And the most amazing part is that you kept our secret!"

I nodded. It had been tough.

Sophia stopped.

"I told my mom," she said.

"Oh my gosh," Bonita and I gasped in unison.

Sophia nodded.

"I told her that I'd come to Princess Allison for help and that you and Mike had planned this great fair to raise funds for Jason. I thought she was going to blow up. But instead she just sat down on the bed and cried. We're a lot alike in that regard. We cry a lot. Then she hugged me, and then she ran into my brother's room and hugged him. She had been really worried. She's a good mom. Really, she is. Sometimes she gets her priorities mixed up, but I think she's seeing things more clearly now."

"What will she tell your dad?"

Sophia shrugged.

"I don't know. Maybe she'll say that she found the money. I don't think she'll tell Daddy the truth."

I put my arm around her. Her world was so complicated. With all the lying and covering up and putting on a happy face for the public. I pointed the three of us from the shade tree toward the food tent. Jennifer and Haley were watching us from a distance, pretending to be in close discussion with three boys I recognized from school. Surprise was written all over their faces.

"Hey, Princess!"

Mike's voice thundered from the direction of the reception desk.

"Wait up!"

I stopped. A couple policemen were jogging beside Mike. In Mike's hand, he held two ropes and appeared to be dragging something behind him. As he got closer, the policemen stepped aside to reveal a wheel chair bumping along behind them. A smiling Jason sat inside, obviously enjoying the ride.

"Oh my god!" gasped Sophia. Forgetting to swish her hair, she raced toward her brother.

"Hey, Sophia! These guys are so cool. I can't believe they put this whole thing on for me! It's incredible!"

Aside from being a little pale, Jason looked the same as he had last year when he graduated from Middle School. He was a cool guy. Instead of looking embarrassed at being pulled around in a wheel chair, he was soaking up all the attention.

"Hey, Princess Allison!" he called to me. "You do good work!"

I froze and kind of smiled, not expecting him to talk to me. I even looked behind me in a stupid move I regretted immediately. As if there'd be someone else around named Princess Allison!

"Yeah, you in the pink shirt. I know who you are. I remember shooting hoops with your dad," Jason said and beamed. I smiled a silky, silly smile back. Boy, he was cute.

Sophia looked terribly confused.

"Jason—how did you get here?"

"I rode with them," Jason said and tossed his head backwards. Sophia's parents approached, walking slowly, arm-in-arm. Her mom was crying, and from this distance, it looked like her father might be crying too.

"Mommy and Daddy!" Sophia squealed, sounding like a little girl and not the Sophia who was so cool and sophisticated. She raced to them and threw her arms around them both. They reached out for her, and folded her into their arms. Her dad placed his hand on her head and mussed her hair.

"I guess this is a private moment," Bonita whispered. "Since no one is paying attention to me, I'm going to sneak into the food tent for some cotton candy."

"But I thought you were all into protein," I laughed.

"There's just so much of that a body can stand. You can't expect me to change overnight!" she said, and ran off. A short distance away, Bonita turned and ran back to Allison's side.

In an elaborate series of motions, Bonita executed a deep curtsy.

"My most highness *Princess Allison the Benevolent*, you have today proven you are deserving of your name and your reputation. It is an honor serving you as Lady in Waiting."

As Mike and his police buddies, and Sophia's family looked on, I helped Bonita to her feet. In a final gesture, we pumped our fists in the air.

"Kids Rule!" we yelled.

J. G. Matheny

Chapter 18
The Renaissance

My loyal subjects of the kingdom of LaPoste, Princess Aqualine the Wise here to proclaim the winner of today's scientific judging in the town square. Sir Michael the Moral and a panel of kingdom experts assessed every entry. Each alchemist displayed immense knowledge of the substance known as Stretchy, and how it might be applied within our kingdom to improve our lives. Everything from covering wagon wheels, to storing food, to blanketing crops against cold. And lest we forget to mention, footwear.

It seems applying the bright colors, I had so much wanted, to my Gators proved too challenging for our alchemists' level of knowledge. Perhaps I am ahead of my time in wanting the colorful Gators. However, the winning alchemist proved his ingenuity, and I will be proudly modeling my new black-and-white striped Gators on my daily outings.

History will credit the winner of today's judging with these amazing contributions. Our own Lady Saraphina's father, Lord Michelin, won the competition. I am only somewhat disappointed that he refuses to call his concoction Stretchy. He prefers our original word, rubber.

Thank you all. I am so proud to be your Princess Aqualine the Wise.

"History will credit you, Princess Aqualine."

"And Sir Michael the Moral, too."

Lady Bonifay nodded. "Yes, and Sir Michael too, for providing this vision and direction. I am truly honored to serve as your Lady in Waiting."

Lady Bonifay curtsied deeply, but tipped sideways while trying to stand up. Princess Aqualine came to her rescue and helped her to her feet.

"Whew! I am terribly sorry, Princess. These winter months I have added too many new pounds to my already ample figure. I am afraid I am getting fat!" Bonifay laughed.

Princess Aqualine hooked arms with her.

"Lady Bonifay, let me tell you about an idea that came to me in my dream a few nights ago. Have you ever heard of something entitled the *food py*ramid?"

Chapter 19

Present day

Good evening loyal subjects. Princess Allison the Benevolent here, checking in for my nightly webcast. I believe that each and every one of my listeners—my loyal subjects—participated in the fair today and brought their friends and family to make it an amazing success.

I wanted to provide a recap of events and some interesting statistics for those of you who enjoy keeping track. We had over 1,500 people attend today! The Fair lasted from ten in the morning right up until bed time. The food ran out sometime in between. I want to thank those mothers and fathers who made some quick grocery runs in the afternoon to sustain this fine repast.

Princess Allison personally witnessed three elementary school children throwing up in the bushes from too many hot dogs and too much Tilt-A-Whirl. I am certain that my loyal subjects saw more, so this number is undoubtedly too low. This is the sign of a good time for kids!

About 500 balloons were donated for the event. The helium ran out and so they had to be blown up by volunteers. My thanks to those who donated their personal wind.

Thousands of dollars were raised to help our loyal subject pay for an important operation. I can't share the exact number, but rest assured it will be enough. What a wonderful realm.

On a personal note, the money raised wasn't the only miracle from this afternoon. Princess Allison the Benevolent witnessed a family mend its priorities. They admitted to being human—to having troubles and needing help. It was amazing to see my loyal subjects' reactions. They didn't make fun of them or turn their backs. In fact, it was the exact opposite. This family learned that honesty was better than keeping secrets, and people can be trusted to understand and help.

I have learned that I have a super family and super friends. Thank you all. I am proud to be your Princess. This is Princess Allison the Benevolent signing off.

The Princess in My Head

J. G. Matheny

PART II
The Screenplay

J. G. Matheny

THE PRINCESS IN MY HEAD

A Play in Two Acts
Run time: Approximately Seventy Minutes

Synopsis: A tale of two princesses influencing their worlds and each other's for the better.

Age Group: Middle grade appeal for screenplay.

Visit ThePrincessInMyHead.com for production ideas and inspiration.

Written by J. G. Matheny
Based on the book by J. G. Matheny

Cast of Characters

The Present

Princess Allison the Benevolent
A young girl with big ideas and a computer

Lady Bonita
Allison's BFF and most loyal subject

Sophia
The most popular girl in school

Sophia's Pack
Sophia's friends and followers in school

Mom
A nice lady who makes great lasagna

Big Mike
A police detective with flaming red hair and beard

Richie Harrell
A funny, farting classmate

Festival Cops
Officers from the LaPoste Police Department

Nerd2Beat's Mother
Festival Attendee

The Renaissance

Princess Aqualine the Wise
A young Renaissance princess

Lady Bonifay
Aqualine's Lady in Waiting and most loyal subject

Lady Saraphina
The most popular girl in the realm

Saraphina's Pack
Saraphina's friends and followers in the realm

Sir Michael the Moral
> A brave knight with flaming red hair and beard

Young Haroldson
> Sir Michael's Page

Lord Michelin
> Saraphina's father

ACT I

Scene 1

Individual lights come on each; Princess Aqualine is in her castle bedroom, speaking to her side of the audience. Allison is dressed in jeans and a T-Shirt, her standard garb; Aqualine wears her Renaissance dress.

AQUALINE

'Tis truly a wonder, this girl I see. So clear she is, like I'm staring into a pool of still water, as if I am looking at myself. But mine eyes behold *such strange and different hair...*

ALLISON

It's really bizarre, I have to admit. It's like my twin took a ride in the hot tub time machine and got stranded in the Renaissance. Don't get me wrong—she's done a good job back there. She's probably only my age, and yet they call her Princess Aqualine *the Wise*.

AQUALINE

And this young girl that I see, as if looking through the

grandest and most perfect
mirror glass, abides in the
strangest world, and I fear
hath the strangest clothing...

ALLISON

Our lives connect when I sleep.
Her Renaissance world invades
my dreams. Her ideas become
mine.

AQUALINE

And I awake with the grandest
of inspirations. Wouldst thou
believe amidst such wondrous
differences, lo, come truly
amazing and useful ideas that
have influenced my kingdom and
made me a beloved princess
here?

ALLISON

Every day Princess Aqualine
writes a letter—a proclamation—
to her loyal subjects in
LaPoste, France that inspires
them...educates them...entertains
them, and every day they gather
in the town square to wait for
it to be posted. When I saw her
doing this, and then I looked
at my super computer here, I
thought, I should do that too.
At least I ought to be able to

inspire my middle school
classmates.

AQUALINE

Her realm too is LaPoste but in
a foreign country titled Wis—
con—sin. Her face reflects as
if in a mirror from a colossal
box!

ALLISON

It is because I see her...

AQUALINE

It is because she is in my
head...

ALLISON

It is because she is in my
head...

AQUALINE

That I know being a Princess
isn't about privilege, it's
about responsibility.

ALLISON

And I can be of help.

AQUALINE

And I can rule.

ALLISON

And we can rule.

Scene 2

Scene: *Modern Day. We see a hall way, a banister, the hall door to Allison's bedroom and the bedroom. On a hall rug at the bottom of the stairs is a giant pair of outdoor boots, a pair of bright Gators and a pair of running shoes. Allison is in her bedroom above. Her twin bed pushed against one wall and a big Teddy Bear on top. A computer with a large screen sits on a desk. Allison wears head phones and is speaking into a microphone.*

ALLISON

Good evening my loyal subjects of LaPoste. *Princess Allison the Benevolent* here, checking in for my nightly webcast. For starters, let me apologize for what I understand is our third solid day of rain *in a row*. It's depressing for *me*, and I know that for you, my loyal subjects, it must be bumming *you* out. It's hard to behave nobly when you're slipping and falling in the mud. Or its splashes up from your bike's back tire making a skunk stripe

from your pants up your
t-shirt. Or it tracks into your
humble homes making your moms
yell. If I could change the
weather, you know that I *would*.
My only wish is for my loyal
subjects to enjoy life as much
as possible. Might I suggest
that everyone buy a pair of
those great rubbery shoes known
as *Gators*? And if they are too
expensive, then I have it on
good authority that the copycat
knockoffs are just as good. Not
only will they protect your
loyal feet better and be more
fashionable, but since they are
made from an oil resin form of
rubber, they wash up so quickly
and easily in a tub of water.

Before I sign off, I am taking
a poll. Today is *Wednesday,* a
day and a word that I love. But
Thursday is not my favorite. I
am considering issuing a royal
edict changing its name to
something more interesting.
Please feel free to submit your
suggestions as I will offer a
prize to whoever is the
cleverest. That's it for now.
Princess Allison the Benevolent
signing off.

MOTHER

J. G. Matheny

(Voice from off stage)

Allison! Bonita's here!

ALLISON

Coming!

(runs to banister and looks over)

Lady Bonita—welcome loyal subject.

BONITA

(looks chubby, wearing cammo pants and an oversized T-Shirt)

Princess Allison, am I too late for the webcast?

ALLISON

Yup. Sorry. Mom had me hurry. She's got a date tonight. Why are you balancing on one foot?

BONITA

My Nikes are muddy and I don't want to mess your Mom's floor. I can't fit my feet on the mat.

ALLISON

So, you'd rather fall on your butt than step off the mat and

mess up my floor. You are
indeed a loyal subject.

(to *Audience*)

Bonita's name means pretty in
Spanish. Reality falls a little
short, as you can see. This is
a state of affairs that isn't
lost on Bonita. That's probably
why she was my most eager
recruit. As a lady in waiting,
I appreciate the beauty of her
soul, and don't get hung up on
the things her mom and dad
always harp on—that roll of
tubbiness around her middle.
Those slightly imperfect teeth.
They're holding braces hostage
right now until she loses
weight. I think that's a
terrible thing to do to an
adolescent. After all, we're
going through the dreaded
puberty and we're all a little
messed up. Can't they show a
little compassion? Maybe
straight teeth are just the
encouragement she needs to take
care of the other perceived
shortcomings. Anyway, as
*Princess Allison the
Benevolent*, I figure its' my
job to take up the slack and
make her feel at least as
beautiful as her name.

(to Bonita)

Did you have an item for the webcast?

BONITA

Not really. I was just thinking we could start our list of weekend activities that don't involve TV.

ALLISON

You are positively obsessed with getting kids away from the TV. When you grow up and run for president, I am sure that issue will top your political platform. But it's a good idea. Maybe we'll do it on tomorrow night's webcast. I talked about muddy feet tonight.

BONITA

(giggling)

If you'll pardon the affront, Princess Allison but don't you think that topic's a little lame?

ALLISON

(moving down the stairs)

Maybe. But I think muddy feet
are on every kid's mind right
now. And I told everyone about
Gators. They're really a
remarkable invention. Take your
shoes off and put them next to
my green Gators. I'll move the
boots. They don't belong here.

BONITA

Whose are they?

ALLISON

Haven't the foggiest. But from
the size of them, we should
call the newspaper. Tell 'em
Bigfoot's been sighted in
LaPoste, Wisconsin. Are you
hungry?

BONITA

(making a face)

Maybe. A little.

ALLISON

Oh, I can tell by that face.
Noodles and applesauce again?

BONITA

Uh-huh.

ALLISON

For *dinner*? You need some protein, Loyal Subject! Doesn't your mom understand the food pyramid? I'll get you some peanut butter and celery.

BONITA

Remember when you covered it in your webcast two months ago? The food pyramid, I mean? I printed it out and left it on the counter for my mom. But I guess she didn't notice. I think my mother wants to starve me. She says noodles will fill me up and I won't eat as much other stuff.

ALLISON

My loyal subjects are being starved to death! And their oppressors are right under the same roof! How *tragic*. We need to repeat the broadcast. Should I make protein an edict?

BONITA

I dunno. Edicts confuse me. What if they're not followed?

ALLISON

I hadn't thought about it.
Edicts are the laws our loyal
subjects must follow. If edicts
aren't followed, then
punishment is called for.

BONITA

Yes, and you're Princess
Allison the *Benevolent*.

ALLISON

Punishing subjects isn't my
thing. Too many edicts could
bring down my monarchy.

BONITA

Maybe. But I wish you could
issue an edict on Sophia and
her *pack*. Man, they make my
life miserable.

ALLISON

You said they've been leaving
you alone lately. What
happened?

BONITA

They have been, except for
today in gym. You know I can't
climb that rope. I was
horrified Miss Amherst made me
try. She's usually on my side.

But I guess there's this fitness test that everyone in the school has to take and, well, I tried. I got up a little far. It wasn't that bad, really, until Sophia started laughing at me. I really hate her. She thinks that just because she has long hair and her mom lets her highlight it so it looks blonde, that she's better than everyone. Then Haley started in too, and you know the boys just follow along because they're so stupid. So, I was stuck on this rope. I was afraid to go down because now everyone was staring and my gym shorts had made a big wedgie...

ALLISON

I hate it when that happens. So, what did you do?

BONITA

Well, I was ready to just open my fists and drop down to the mat, but I was afraid I'd sprain an ankle...

ALLISON

Sophia can be so mean...

BONITA

Yeah...you know that better than anybody. But then Richie Harrell—he was next in line—farted really loud and everyone laughed and in the confusion, I kind of wiggled down. When it was his turn, he kept farting really loud all the way up the rope and everyone went crazy. Can you imagine? I think he was doing it on purpose to get attention. Anyway, they forgot about me and my wedgie. How'd you do?

ALLISON

Oh, you know...Most of the kids in my class are nice.

BONITA

Yeah, you lucked out getting fifth period gym. But I mean how did you do? Did you set another school record or something? Did you make it to the top in like...five seconds?

ALLISON

If you must know, it took me thirty-five seconds. Up and down and that was it. No biggie.

BONITA

You're amazing. If I was like you and could do five hundred sit ups and a million push-ups, I'd be pretty stuck up but you're not.

ALLISON

I'm a benevolent princess, so I simply can't act stuck up about something as silly as gym. Let's get upstairs. I'll playback tonight's webcast and we can pick some topics for tomorrow. I'm thinking of changing the name for Thursday.

BONITA

What should I do with my muddy Nikes?

ALLISON

You should get some *Gators*.

Scene 3

A castle bedroom with a draped bed and a writing desk that holds a vat of ink and a candle for light. Aqualine wakes up, stretches and walks to the desk. Sits for a moment and then dips her quill pen into the ink vat and begins to write on a large piece of parchment *paper.*

AQUALINE

(speaking as she writes)

Welcome loyal subjects to today's proclamation. On this wonderful April day in the year of Our Lord 1590, Princess Aqualine the Wise wishes you to know about something vitally important that came to me in my dreams last night. I know these constant days of rain have been disheartening for us all, but they can be rendered easier if we protect our feet with a brightly colored covering. We can make these coverings of a pliable fabric called rubber that keeps the wet out but is also very easy to clean.

I will dub these new items *Gators*. I know that this is a funny, unfamiliar word, but since the Renaissance spirit now engages us all, why not embrace something new? The bright color is extremely important because the *Gators* must be made in green, orange, pink and purple. Wouldn't that be lively?

Before I dip my quill into my

berry juice vat to sign off for
today, I am also thinking of
issuing an edict to change the
name for Thursday to another,
more beautiful word. As always,
your beloved Princess Aqualine
the Wise is open to your
suggestions on this topic. Good
day.

BONIFAY

(enters bed chamber carrying a gown)

Milady, your cheerfulness
baffles me. How can you think
this to be a wonderful April
day? What with the chilly
mustiness inside the castle
walls. Days like this make me
miserable!

AQUALINE

I was just too excited, Lady
Bonifay! What say you of my
idea?

BONIFAY

If you'll pardon the dissent,
Princess Aqualine, this idea is
rather ambitious even for you.
And how should your loyal
subjects obtain these Gators?

AQUALINE

I believe that I should offer a
reward to whomever in the
kingdom can develop the
formula. There is little to go
on, I realize, however I know
that it is a mysterious,
stretchable fabric made with
resin. It resists water and
cleans quickly so it will make
the most glorious shoes!

BONIFAY

Once again, Milady, if you'll
pardon the question. Do you
truly think it is worth your
subject's time to invent this
new substance when it's only
purpose would be to make
brightly colored foot wear?

AQUALINE

I know it sounds a little
silly.

BONIFAY

You know the Lady Saraphina
will be standing by to make
fun. This is just the kind of
idea that she will scoff.

AQUALINE

Such as she did with my warm

jumper idea.

*(rummages and picks up a crude but
recognizable adaptation of a Snuggly)*

BONIFAY

Exactly. When you first
insisted upon calling it a
Snuggly. And the early woolen
weavings proved itchy, not
snuggly at all.

AQUALINE

Yes, coming up with just the
right fabric blend proved more
difficult. But now they are
quite popular for sitting
before the fire.

BONIFAY

I only wish to protect you from
ridicule, my princess. Lady
Saraphina is popular within the
realm with those who wish only
to parade their clothes and go
to balls. Remember the mean
words when you suggested your
top of the lap desk?

AQUALINE

Lap top desk. You have to say
the words in that order. But I
truly believe that once we have

this substance, this *rubber*, we can use it for our floors and our roofs so that they don't leak.

BONIFAY

(*giggling*)

But the castle's roofs don't leak often. We can walk easily around the entire yard and never get wet. We are protected by the wooden awnings. I can carry an umbrella for you when you cross the pathways, and have clean slippers ready for you on the other side. You are a princess after all.

AQUALINE

But being a princess in this Renaissance time isn't about privilege. It's about responsibility. I have to take care of my loyal subjects and make their lives easier. It doesn't matter that I am comfortable if my subjects are wet and cold and suffering.

Scene 4

Inside Allison's modern-day bedroom. Bonita sits on the bed playing with a teddy bear.

Allison at her desk. They take up their conversation where left off.

BONITA

If you'll pardon the affront, Princess Allison, but you could be popular like Sophia if you tried. Lots of kids know you. They listen to your webcasts. They think you're really smart and helpful. And if your mom let you grow your hair longer and get your ears pierced...

ALLISON

Lady Bonita, I like my hair short. It doesn't flop in my face when I run. If I were popular then I'd spend all my time trying to stay popular and wondering what people think of me and why "Jennifer" didn't call me like she said she would, and all that crazy stuff. I have other things on my mind. Like why your mother thinks it's motivational not to feed you.

BONITA

Okay, you're right. Besides, if you were popular, I probably wouldn't be your friend.

ALLISON

You'll always be my friend.

BONITA

But Princess Allison, you have the power to be popular but you don't choose to be.

ALLISON

You have the power, too. You're not stuck with your current social standing.

BONITA

I disagree.

ALLISON

(*sighing*)

I know.

MOM

(*Standing outside door with Mike—a very tall man with red hair and beard. She knocks*)

Allison, open the door, honey. We're about to leave for the movie. I wanted you to meet Mike.

ALLISON

(Opens door and they walk in)

ALLISON and BONITA

Oh my gosh! Wow!

MOM

This is Mike..

BONITA

(whispering)

That's the most enormous man
I've ever seen. Look at that
red beard!

ALLISON

(whispering)

It's *Bigfoot.*

MOM

You get this reaction a lot,
Mike?

BIG MIKE

(good natured laugh)

Yeah, it happens. Hi Allison.
Hi Bonita. Did I hear her call
you *Princess* Allison?

BONITA

(to Allison)

Oh, no, here it comes!

MOM

Yes, Allison is *Princess* of her middle school land and Bonita is her *lady in waiting*. See over there? She's got her computer set up with a microphone and camera, and they do a nightly webcast to the kingdom, which is actually most of our neighborhood. Allison, Mike is a police detective.

BONITA

She's Princess Allison *the Benevolent*.

ALLISON

(aside)

Look—He's not even noticing us. He's making goo-goo eyes at my mom. Yuck!

(talking louder)

Being a Princess isn't about privilege. It's about

responsibility.

BONITA

Princess Allison takes care of
the loyal subjects in her
kingdom. She *rules*.

BIG MIKE

Yeah, I know. *Kids rule.*

(giving them a fist salute)

MOM

We'll be home about eleven.
We're just doing a quick dinner
and movie. You'll be just fine.

*Mike offers them another fist salute and he
and Mom exit.*

BONITA

How sad. He doesn't get it.
He's an amazingly huge man with
an important job, but he still
doesn't get it.

ALLISON

Right. I think I'm destined for
something pink the next time he
comes over. Again.

BONITA

All your mom's boyfriends miss
the point, don't they?

ALLISON

Yup. They sure do.

Scene 5

*Aqualine's Renaissance bedroom. Bonifay is
braiding Aqualine's hair. She and Lady Bonifay
resume conversation. She holds up the
completed daily proclamation.*

BONIFAY

But rubber? That is such an
ugly word. Perhaps we should
change it, if it is really to
become a revolutionary
substance?

AQUALINE

Hmm. *Rubber* was the word that
had come in the royal dream but
'tis rather awkward. Saying it
aloud makes my lips pop.

BONIFAY

Yay, 'tis undignified for a
princess. And pray tell me what
indeed is being rubbed?

AQUALINE

What may we call it? 'Tis
pliable and moldable and
stretchable to cover surfaces
to make them waterproof.
Perhaps molder? Royal molder
pliant? Nay, that name does not
sing.

BONIFAY

(*clapping hands*)

Or *Stretchy*! Dost thou not see?
It will be as your Snuggly
name. Only Stretchy! It is
lyrical.

AQUALINE

Perchance a more dignified
name, Lady Bonifay?

BONIFAY

(*disappointed*)

Princess, you are the clever
and wise one. I will leave you
to work on its name.

AQUALINE

Actually, Lady Bonifay,
although so many give me credit
for my clever ideas, I fear I

am not that clever.

BONIFAY

Why they call you Aqualine the
wise.

AQUALINE

I have developed a reputation
around the countryside as the
wise little princess. Finally,
something to be known for other
than the little sister to the
future king. But I am not that
wise. I owe so many of my ideas
to the little princess in my
royal dream. When my dream
washed over me last night and
the puffy clouds parted in my
mind, I saw her so clearly. As
though she were on stage and I
in her audience. Her hair and
costumes are much different.
And her means of delivering
proclamations so odd. But her
guidance is remarkable. By the
way, what do you think of my
changing the name for Thursday?
It's a good idea?

BONIFAY

Well, actually Princess
Aqualine, if you'll pardon the
opposition, I think Thursday is
the best name in the entire

week. It is named for *Thor*. He
was a giant god with red hair
and a flowing beard who
protected an entire kingdom. If
you take away his day, he just
may take away his protection
and we really need it in this
uncertain time.

AQUALINE

Oh, you are right Lady Bonifay.
So many times, you have kept me
from doing something foolish. I
do appreciate your counsel. I
also appreciate your braiding
ability. You work magic on my
unruly hair. What do you
suppose I would look like if I
cut it short?

BONIFAY

(giggling)

Why would you wish to do that,
Milady?

AQUALINE

It is just an idea.

*Bonifay takes proclamation and begins to roll
it up.*

BONIFAY

Then you would look like *Prince*

Aqualine.

AQUALINE

Don't roll that proclamation
just yet. I must cross
something out. There.

Thursday will stay as it was.

BONIFAY

Thor will be pleased.

Scene 6

*In the town square. Aqualine and Bonifay
attach the proclamation to a pillar.
Townspeople mill around. Lady Saraphina, a
pretty girl with long hair walks forward. She
is followed by two or three other girls
hovering closely.*

SARAPHINA

Oh, what are we proclaiming
today, Princess Aqualine?
Another crazy idea? And Lady
Bonifay following along
blindly, as usual.

AQUALINE

Lady Saraphina, you are welcome
to challenge my proclamations
but not my loyal lady in

131

waiting. You and your pack may take your leave if you have nothing happy to say.

SARAPHINA

Me and my...what foreign term dost thou use? My *pack*?

AQUALINE

(suddenly embarrassed)

I...I know not where that came from.

BONIFAY
(rising to her defense)

Yes, your *pack*, Lady Saraphina. Alone you are each like a castle pet, quiet and companionable and able to do little harm. But together you are as a pack of dogs barking loudly and wreaking havoc.

SARAPHINA

(reading the proclamation and giggling)

You believe someone in this kingdom should develop this ugly thing you call rubber and adapt it for garish shoes? What a waste of our time. Why don't you plan a ball instead?

Something fun that your loyal
subjects will enjoy.

*All the towns people look to her. They seem to
like the idea of a ball.*

AQUALINE

(defensively)

Being a princess is not about
going to balls and such
frivolity. I must lead my loyal
subjects.

BONIFAY

Yes, she must *rule*.

*A tall man dressed as a knight with a red
beard approaches the group.*

SIR MICHAEL

(pumping his fist in the air)

Princess Aqualine Rules!

AQUALINE

*(surprised and a little
intimidated)*

Sir Michael, 'tis a surprise to
see you here.

SIR MICHAEL

Lady Bonifay. Princess. I see that you are inspiring your realm again.

AQUALINE

I try but it seems that many scoff. Dost thou scoff too?

SIR MICHAEL

(stroking his beard in thought)

To me you will always be little Princess Aqua tagging along behind your older brothers. But such memory is now a disservice. You are indeed an unusual young woman with ambitious ideas.

BONIFAY

So thou dost support Princess Aqualine?

SIR MICHAEL

I honor thy efforts.

AQUALINE

(somewhat acidly)

'Tis not the same. But I know I

hang low on the royal ladder
you must climb.

SIR MICHAEL

Not true, but unfortunately my
actions now will not comfort
you. I must away to the castle
as your brothers and the Queen
have summoned me.

Sir Michael bows and departs.

BONIFAY

Milady, you should be nicer.

AQUALINE

I fear he neither understands
me nor appreciates my
proclamations. To him I am only
baby Princess Aqua.

BONIFAY

I implore you to be more
patient with Sir Michael. He is
a grand knight of the realm and
could be a big help to you. In
fact, he doth remind me of
Thor, what with his red hair
and beard.

AQUALINE

But you must agree. Of my

ideas, he is highly skeptical.

BONIFAY

He is a wise man and he wonders
from whence the ideas come. To
him, as to us all they seem
equal part genius and wizardry.

AQUALINE

Do you, Lady Bonifay, worry
from whence they come?

BONIFAY

No, Princess, I have great
faith in you. Your dreams
deliver ideas that help, and
often make me laugh. I do not
worry. But I do wonder.

They exit.

Scene 7

*The next day. Allison sits before her computer
wearing headphones and speaking into the
microphone. Bonita sits on the bed reading a
book.*

ALLISON

Good evening loyal subjects.
Princess Allison the Benevolent
here, checking in for my

nightly webcast. For starters
tonight, I am so happy that
many of you felt the advice on
Gators worthwhile. My blog has
registered quite a few
comments. Heather from Crescent
Street says she wishes there
were *Gators* for dogs. I guess
her Lab has made a real mess of
the stairway carpet and the
Jeep's upholstery. Bummer.

On my other topic from last
night—when I proposed changing
the name for Thursday? Well,
I'm re-thinking this idea. It
seems Thursday is named after
this amazing warrior god *Thor*
who is known for protecting
entire kingdoms and children.
He is much more than a Marvel
comic. So, if we remove *Thor's*
day, we might lose his
protection. And I think any
protection, even mythical, in
these uncertain times is a good
thing. As I am willing to admit
publicly my mistakes, I hope
that you will all take this as
example and be willing to admit
when you are wrong. It doesn't
hurt. That's it for now.
*Princess Allison the Benevolent
signing off.*

BONITA

I think it's important that you admitted you were wrong to change Thursday. *Thor* was such an amazing guy! It says here he could bring animals back to life. That's my favorite part. I wish he'd been around for my cat K.C. You know, *Thor* reminds me of...

ALLISON

(covering her ears)

Don't say it!

BONITA

No, Allison. You have to listen. He reminds me of Mike— the guy your Mom is dating? Mike is just huge, like *Thor*. And the red beard and hair— whoa! Come on—it occurred to you, too, right? And he's a detective—that's a protector of justice, right? Mike could be a modern-day *Thor*.

ALLISON

I know...I have to admit the similarity did occur to me.

BONITA

Princess Allison, if you'll

pardon the affront, I think you
should give Mike a
chance. He brought you that
cool scarf and the diary today.
At least he's trying.

*Bonita holds up an over-the-top pink scarf and
furry book.*

ALLISON

Bonita, the scarf is *pink* and
the diary is covered in *fur*.
They look like souvenirs from
Disney World. Then he did that
lame *Kids Rule* fist salute
again.

(mimicing the salute)

BONITA

Well, if you'll *again* pardon
the contradiction, Princess
Allison, not everyone has been
to Disney World. I haven't. And
souvenirs from there sound like
something special to me. I
happen to like Disney, and I
wouldn't mind it if someone
bought me a scarf or a diary
from their store. I wouldn't
care if it was covered in fur.
That seems kind of nice,
actually. The only presents I
get these days are *Healthy
Gourmet* frozen dinners and

brochures for fat camp.

ALLISON

Oh, Bonita... I'm sorry.

BONITA

Allison, sometimes you behave like a princess—and not a noble one. I like being your Lady in Waiting when you are doing important things, and thinking grand thoughts for the common good, but when you start on about your mother's boyfriends and how they treat you, well, let's just say you're less benevolent in my eyes.

ALLISON

Wow. I hadn't thought about things that way. Okay. What if Mike is really a modern-day protector in our kingdom?

BONITA

Then that would make you wrong, and you'd owe him an apology. And you'd have to pledge to be nicer because you might actually need him.

ALLISON

But I don't think I need saving
and protecting.

BONITA

Then maybe he's like Thor and
here to protect your realm.
Maybe he's going to battle for
somebody we know.

ALLISON

Hmmm. Maybe. It's worth
considering.

BONITA

(squealing)

Oh, my gosh! I almost forgot! I
have to tell you something!

ALLISON

I'm still trying to imagine
Mike as a modern-day Thor. I
can't get beyond his big feet.
Did Thor have big feet?

BONITA

Forget that. This is really
incredible. You won't believe
who came up to me in school
today!

Scene 8

School Hall. Bonita is stopped by Sophia with long hair and the latest fashion. Sophia signals her.

SOPHIA

Hey. Come 'ere.

BONITA

What? Who? Me?

SOPHIA

Yes, you. You're Lady Bonita, right?

BONITA

Well, yeah. I didn't know you knew.

SOPHIA

Of course, I know. You're Lady in Waiting to Princess Allison.

BONITA

Princess Allison *the Benevolent.*

SOPHIA

Sure. Whatever. Listen, I'm
sorry about yesterday and that
rope thing. We shouldn't have
laughed at you.

BONITA

Then why did you?

SOPHIA

Oh, I don't know. Sometimes
when there's lots of people
around, I just do things like
that.

BONITA

To get attention? It was pretty
mean and I didn't like it.

SOPHIA

I'm sorry, okay? But now I just
need to talk to you. I know
some kids who listen to your
webcasts. They like them.

BONITA

Really? Kids that hang with
you? That's *extreme*!

SOPHIA

Well, sort of. I was just
wondering how it all worked.

How you pick your topics.

BONITA

Well we... Princess Allison and I...want to inspire kids to be better citizens of our realm.

SOPHIA

And where is your realm?

BONITA

Well, basically it's just here in LaPoste. And it's just basically kids our age.

Parents are well-meaning, but kids can inspire each other better sometimes. And that's why *Princess Allison the Benevolent* gives guidance to make good decisions and act less selfishly.

SOPHIA

So how many kids listen?

BONITA

We had forty-eight last night. It was a new record. But our audience is bigger than that since not everyone can listen every night. So maybe double that? Maybe triple?

SOPHIA

No, I think you're wrong.

BONITA

(hesitant)

If you'll pardon the disagreement, Sophia. That's what I say to Princess Allison, if all you want to do is make me feel bad again, then I'm going to go...

SOPHIA

Oh, no! That's not it, Bonita! I'm sorry. What I mean is I think you have a lot more listeners. I've been asking around and everyone knows about you and Princess Allison and your webcasts and how much you like Gators and that kind of stuff. I want to ask you something.

BONITA

Well, okay. What?

SOPHIA

Will you tell Princess Allison

to meet me tomorrow in the
library after lunch? I think,
well, you know. Maybe I, uh, I
might need her help.

*Sophia departs. Boy comes from out of the
shadows.*

RICHIE HARRELL

That was so cool!

BONITA

You were spying on us?

RICHIE HARRELL

Yeah, well. I had on my cloak
of invisibility and nobody saw.
That was the *bomb*! Sophia likes
you and Princess Allison.

BONITA

I know, er, I guess. But it's
okay. I like it.

RICHIE HARRELL

It's awesome! But I always knew
you guys were pretty cool.

BONITA

Really? You did?

They exit, talking.

Scene 9

In the school library. Toadstool chairs are set side by side. Allison is alone idly walking around, grabbing books from the shelf, glancing at them then putting them back. She is wearing a hoody and jeans, waiting for Sophia to join her.

ALLISON

(to audience)

So here I am in the library waiting for Sophia. If I were a loyal subject, what advice would I give myself? How should I act around someone who had once been a really close friend, and then grew up to be such a snob? Since I call myself the benevolent, I am probably stuck with acting that way. Do you know that I started my webcasts because of Sophia? I wanted to help kids deal with a Sophia in their lives, and I wanted to somehow influence them not to become like her.

I'd read a story about *Princess Aqualine the Wise* and how she issued daily proclamations that helped her kingdom. Back then

life was so strict and people
were so angry. Princess
Aqualine led her loyal subjects
into the Renaissance when
music, art and happiness
flourished. She was just my age
when she started her messages
to her kingdom.

So, I thought what if I did my
own proclamations? Dad set up
my computer for webcasts and
then the magic started and I
began hearing Princess Aqualine
in my dreams. I didn't worry
about Sophia after that. Until
now, of course.

Sophia enters.

ALLISON

Look, there she is. Can you
believe it? She's wearing flip
flops? Who wears flip flops in
Wisconsin during the Spring
rainy season? But they do look
pretty cool with her leggings
and her yellow cashmere sweater
really is pretty. My humble
jeans and hoody pale in
comparison.

(to Sophia)

Where are your *Gators?*

SOPHIA

Oh yeah. Oh well, these are
prettier.

ALLISON

Sometimes that's not the point.

SOPHIA

No. Sometimes that's not *your*
point. My point is always to be
prettier.

ALLISON

But don't you think there are
other considerations? Like
comfort and whether you'll
catch cold when it rains and
get your feet wet?

SOPHIA

Those are considerations for
you, Ally. You can wear jeans
and that sweatshirt you have on
today because they make sense.
I have to decide my clothes,
and, well, everything else
because they look pretty.

ALLISON

You haven't called me Ally in a
long time. Not since we were

best friends.
It's just that on my webcast
this week I suggested kids wear
Gators to keep their feet dry
and not ruin their other shoes.
I like your flip flops, but
they'd get soaked walking to
the bus and the leather would
crinkle.

SOPHIA

My mom picks me up.

ALLISON

That's right. Normal kids take
the bus. Your mom picks you up
in that big SUV. I just
mentioned the webcast because
Bonita told me you were asking
questions...

SOPHIA

Lady Bonita, right? That's what
you call her? And you're
*Princess Allison the
Benevolent*?

ALLISON

It's not like we're cartoon
characters, Sophia. My teachers
don't call me princess. It's
just who we are each night. And
kids text us messages with

their concerns and tune in to
hear advice. And I, well...
Princess Allison... tries hard to
make it fair and helpful advice
that encourages kids to be
honest and good citizens.

SOPHIA

Do you think I'm a good
citizen?

ALLISON

Actually, I spend some of my
time counseling kids how to
ignore people like you and take
you less seriously. But that's
usually one-on-one advice and
not on the webcast. More
personal, you know.

SOPHIA

Thanks. I suppose it would be
pretty obvious who you were
talking about if you did it on
the webcast.

ALLISON

You are rather...

SOPHIA

Popular?

ALLISON

Notorious.

SOPHIA

Do you ever have guests?

ALLISON

It's really not an interview
program. I suppose we could but
we haven't before.

SOPHIA

But you could?

ALLISON

It would depend on what the
guest would say. Do you want to
be a guest, Sophia?

SOPHIA

Maybe. I need to reach a lot of
people and I just don't know
the best way to do it.

ALLISON

(idea dawns)

Gosh Sophia, you can't use my
webcast to run for *Yearbook*!
It's not that kind of forum! I

can't believe you'd even think
to ask me.

SOPHIA

(starting to cry)

Oh no, Ally. That's not it. I
can't blame you for thinking
the worst of me, but really, I
need it for a good cause. A
really good cause. Nobody at
school knows about it yet.
We've been keeping it a secret
at home but I heard my parents
talking the other night and
they're at the end of their
rope. Then I got the idea that
maybe *Princess Allison the
Benevolent* could help.

(whispering)

My dad lost his job last year.
We had to swear to keep it a
secret. I thought everything
was going okay until I heard
talk about losing the house and
the cars. Anyway, my brother
couldn't try out for High
School football this year. My
mom was worried he might get
injured and we don't have
medical insurance any more. You
know, because my dad lost his
job? And for some reason…and I
don't know why…Dad can't find

another one.

ALLISON

I heard Jason couldn't play
football because he got bad
grades.

SOPHIA

That's what he wanted people to
believe, but his grades are
great. Mom was just terrified
that he'd get hurt. But now he
needs an operation! Nobody's
telling me what's wrong—but I
know it's serious. First, I
overheard my mom and dad
fighting about it. Then mom
started acting strange and
scared. At first, I thought she
was just being cranky. Then
she'd yell at us for no reason
and then run upstairs to cry. I
thought that was just because
of having no money and being so
worried. Mom and I used to go
shopping a lot together and
we'd spend lots of money on
clothes and shoes. We haven't
been able to do that anymore. I
tried once. I took her credit
card and went to the mall with
Jennifer but the store said the
card wasn't any good and I had
to put all the clothes back.
And I really needed them.

ALLISON

We're talking about your mom,
remember?

SOPHIA

Oh, yeah. I heard her on the
phone yesterday. I think she
was talking to the doctor's
office. Jason had some tests
done. Something is wrong with
his legs. Anyway, she kept
telling the doctor's office,
No. There's no money. Then she
hung up and laid down on the
kitchen floor in a ball and
just cried and cried and cried.
It was so awful.

ALLISON

Oh my gosh. Can't they borrow
some money? Like from a bank?

SOPHIA

Uh-uh. My dad can't get any
money from the bank because he
owes so much anyway.

ALLISON

How about from friends or your
grandparents?

SOPHIA

Oh no! That's the worst part.
This is all a *secret*. We can't
tell anybody anything! My dad
would go crazy if he knew I was
telling you. He says the money
problems are a family matter
and we'll handle it ourselves.
So, we can't borrow any money
from people because then the
neighbors would know my dad
lost his job and we weren't
being the way we're supposed to
be.

ALLISON

Well, what is that, exactly?
The way you're supposed to be?

SOPHIA

We're supposed to be rich and
fabulous.

ALLISON

Okay. So, who really cares if
you're not?

SOPHIA

Oh Ally...Don't you know? Really?

ALLISON

No. I don't know. Really.

SOPHIA

Everybody cares. If people knew my dad was broke and couldn't get a job, and if we lost our house and our cars, do you think I'd still be the coolest girl in the school like I am now? Do you think people would still want to be friends with me?

Sophia sobs. Allison hugs her awkwardly. Sophia clings to her and wraps her arms around her as the curtain falls.

J. G. Matheny

ACT 2
Scene 1

Renaissance Time. Aqualine is seated at her desk, inking another proclamation. Lady Bonifay is trying to braid her hair while she writes.

AQUALINE

(speaking as she writes)

My loyal subjects, welcome to today's declaration. So strong a passion doth engulf me, and pray thou as well, for our kingdom's alchemists labor now. My Gators are their prize. But greater riches for our realm they see as that resin concoction will waterproof our roof tops and outdoor clothing to protect ourselves. One noble alchemist hath proclaimed that this rubber first comes from a plant that grows afar. Our mixologists magically combine this wondrous substance to fashion into footwear or spread upon our roofs. Such wonderment!

Most excellent accomplishments, what? Think thee of all the sickness and disease to never

plague our people. Think thee
that rather dry and warm might
be their fate? To know not of
roofs that leak? To know not of
musty and moldy clothing? The
wee babes of my kingdom with no
coughs that last for days and
weeks wracking their little
bodies until weak and feverish?
I say this concoction may be
our gift, our world to better.
Pray, lend me your thoughts at
my castle's suggestion box.
Adieux.

(to Bonifay)

Oh, Lady Bonifay, dost thou
think I am daft putting people
to such work to have my
brightly colored footwear?

BONIFAY
Milady, I am your most loyal
servant...

AQUALINE

I know thou art, but you would
tell me truly what you think?

BONIFAY

It is only that some scoff at
the idea. As always, they are
led by Lady Sarafina, the most
vocal and shrill. She has taken

to calling you Aqualine the
Silly instead of Aqualine the
Wise...

AQUALINE

Oh, it is so hard to lead with
an idea such as this one. I
know it is truly *out there*... (Yet
more words that have taken into
me from my dreams). I believe
in my heart that if we have
faith and try, we will
transform our life.

BONIFAY

If you will grant my open
tongue...

AQUALINE

Of course, speak.

BONIFAY

I embraced your Snuggly idea
when it came unto you, and I
cut the first patterns from the
canvas cloth before we realized
we needed to craft them from
warmer and cozier weavings, and
my father met with such trials
constructing your top of the
lap desk. It was uncomfortable
and slid quickly off your
skirts.

AQUALINE

Ah, but these were helpful ideas...and it's *lap top desk*.

BONIFAY

Oh Milady, you are beloved as smart and innovative. But this idea. It is very big and many are now counting on its success. If it is half as successful as the Snuggly, then so many lives will be transformed. Feet will be dry.

AQUALINE

Do you worry that it might fail?

BONIFAY

I know that my dear father is trying his own concoction. He is excited and intent on succeeding but he has started two fires so far in our house trying to heat the material to a consistency that will stretch and wrap to make a shoe.

AQUALINE

But he is a baker!

BONIFAY

Who better to work with
chemistry?

AQUALINE

Have Lady Saraphina and her
pack been cruel?

BONIFAY

She called you a *child*. She
said that you are playing with
dolls and diverting our realm's
alchemists from our real
problems to make *doll shoes*.

AQUALINE:

Do you believe she has
followers?

BONIFAY

Ah, but yes, some.

AQUALINE

Do you believe me, Lady
Bonifay? Please believe me.

BONIFAY

As you would say, Princess,
this rubber is really *out*
there. But I do. And if you

succeed with this idea, you
need not worry about nay-sayers
and scoffers for ever after.

Scene 2

*Modern day—Allison's bedroom. Allison
broadcasts from her computer and Bonita sits
on the bed.*

ALLISON

Good evening loyal subjects.
Princess Allison the Benevolent
here, checking in for my
nightly webcast. We've made it
through the soggy week and I
promise this weekend will be
more fun. Make a list of those
things you would like to do
outdoors, and I challenge you
all to pledge to do them before
the weekend is over. I know
that I am not alone in
recalling sitting in front of
the window, watching the
perpetual rain and saying to
myself, "If only it were sunny.
I would be riding my bike." Or,
"If only the rain would stop, I
would run next door and see
what those kids were doing."

Well, the time is now. The rain
has stopped. So, let's roll off
that couch and find our legs.

Vow to run out the front door—
letting it slam if it must—and
catapult yourself to the seat
of your trusty bike and ride
out to explore! Imagine that
you were living in the year
1590 and there were no bikes.
Only rain and disease and work.
Celebrate the fact that you
don't live then, and that you
live now!

Before I sign off tonight, I
want to talk about setting
priorities. I know you've heard
this from your parents before,
but it makes sense. If our
priorities are in order, then
everything is fine. But if our
priorities get out of order,
then everything can get messed
up. I met this week with a
loyal subject whose family
priorities are severely out of
whack.

For those of you listening, I
think that we can help our
fellow loyal subject fix her
priorities. Send *Princess
Allison the Benevolent* a
message on our blog right now.
Think very carefully and tell
us the things that are most
important to you in your lives.
Be wise and thoughtful. I know
many of you value your *XBox* and

Smartphones. That's not what we're looking for here. Extra Benevolent points will be awarded to the loyal subject truly understanding this assignment and delivering to me some good ideas. *Princess Allison the Benevolent signing off.*

BONITA

If you'll pardon the affront, Princess Allison, but that last part didn't make much sense. You had me confused, and when I'm confused, our loyal subjects generally are too. The responses are going to suck. Why can't you tell me what this is all about? Maybe I could help.

ALLISON

I can't tell you just yet.

BONITA

Does this have something to do with you and Sophia meeting today? You've been acting really strangely ever since.

ALLISON

Okay Bonita. I was going to
tell you as soon as I figured
out what to do.

BONITA

It is about Sophia, isn't it?
Did she make fun of *Princess
Allison*? Something inside of me
said she was setting you up.

ALLISON

No, she didn't make fun. I
thought she might, too. I could
have fallen on my butt with
surprise when I found out. She
needs our *help*. I mean, she
needs *Princess Allison's* help.

BONITA

Oh my gosh. What for?

ALLISON

Her brother needs an operation.
Her dad's out of a job and they
can't afford to pay for it
because the operation is too
expensive. Her mom cries all
the time because she is so
worried. They're not allowed to
tell anybody about their money
problems. It's this big family
secret. But Sophia thinks that
if her brother doesn't get the

operation, he'll never play
sports again. And her mom and
dad will stay so worried and
upset that they'll break up.
And then, basically, she'd turn
out like me. Personally, I
think that's what scares her
the most.

BONITA

That's crazy. They have that
big house and those really cool
cars. And Sophia's clothes...

ALLISON

She's been going to *Goodwill*
and shopping *EBAY*. She sells
the clothes she grows out of
and buys replacement ones for
her and her mom. They haven't
had any money for a really long
time.

BONITA

But her *pack*? They're all
really rich. They'd figure it
out, you'd think?

ALLISON

She knew she'd be discovered
eventually. After all, the good
stuff at *Goodwill* gets picked
over really quick. Even if you

are a good shopper.

BONITA

So, you feel sorry for Sophia?

ALLISON

Yeah, I guess I do.

BONITA

(suddenly angry)

You can't feel sorry for her!
She's just getting what's
coming to her. So, what if her
pack learns she's broke and
they kick her out? She's mean
and she's selfish. All those
things Princess Allison teaches
her loyal subjects *not* to be.
Sophia never needed you until
there was something you could
do for her!

ALLISON

Oh, no! That's not it, Bonita.
Why are you so upset?

BONITA

(holding Mr. Teddy Boo and
almost sobbing)

I don't know. Exactly. I'm

trying to figure that out.

ALLISON

Princess Allison helps kids,
Bonita. Sometimes things upset
me, too, but I have to stop and
think, and try to put my own
silly concerns aside to be the
voice of *Princess Allison the
Benevolent*. In this case, I
think being benevolent means to
be compassionate. Sophia has
been mean and selfish. I agree.
But she's in a bad situation
now. You can't blame her for
being so status conscious. Look
at her parents! They want to
pretend to the world that
they're still better than
everybody else, when in fact
they have problems just like
normal people. And they force
their kids to keep their secret
and not ask for any help. If
Sophia's parents made family
their priority instead of
status, Sophia would be getting
guidance and strength from
them.

BONITA

So, since her parents are
messing up their priorities,
Sophia needs to find this
guidance and strength somewhere

else. And so, she came to you.

ALLISON

She came to *Princess Allison
the Benevolent* and her awesome
Lady in Waiting. She came to
us. Come on. Let's check the
blog to see if our loyal
subjects sent us any responses.

BONITA

Okay.

ALLISON

What do you think Sophia would
be like if she wasn't, well…
Sophia?

BONITA

You mean if she was more like a
normal kid?

ALLISON

Yeah.

BONITA

Well, honestly, I'd like to say
that nobody would like her and
she wouldn't have any friends,
but Princess Allison the
Benevolent would object to that

kind of wishful thinking.

ALLISON

Ummm. Princess Allison would say you were being envious and selfish.

BONITA

Okay. So, I think Sophia is really pretty. She'd still be popular because she is so pretty. She'd probably have to work harder at it, though. No money for highlights and pedicures and clothes. She'd need to be friendlier, too, since fans just won't drop into her lap like before. Maybe she would be sporty instead of stuck up.

ALLISON

Sophia is good at basketball and volleyball.

BONITA

Ugh. She'd have to change her attitude, though. The last time we played volleyball in gym, Sophia and her pack wouldn't touch the ball because it might break a fingernail. I'd work really hard to bump it up to

one of them, and they'd let it
go *plop*, right in front of the
net. Not even try to get it.

ALLISON

She would have to try harder.

BONITA

So, what exactly did she want
Princess Allison to do to help
her out?

ALLISON

To begin with, she wanted to
appear with me on the webcast,
and just ask kids to contribute
to a really good cause.

BONITA

Oh my gosh. That would make her
look like *Saint* Sophia, looking
out for the underprivileged.
She wasn't going to tell them,
I presume, that she was the
good cause?

ALLISON

I told her that we don't
usually have guests, and it
would be easier to protect her
privacy if Princess Allison
handled it alone.

BONITA

That was diplomatic. Why does
she need privacy?

ALLISON

Her priorities are still messed
up. She wants to help Jason get
money for his operation without
letting anyone know about the
family's money situation.
Sophia wants to keep the
secret.

BONITA

She won't be able to. Word will
get out.

ALLISON

I think maybe we have to ease
her into doing the right thing.
To show her that everything
won't collapse if the secret
gets out. That kids can be
trusted to understand and help.

BONITA

So that's why you had our loyal
subjects send in their list of
priorities!

ALLISON

Yup. I'm thinking we'll show
her some of the responses and
maybe she can talk to her mom
and dad and convince them
people really don't care about
status. That kids care about
more important things.

BONITA

If you'll pardon the affront
once more, Princess Allison, I
really don't think that's the
help Sophia is looking for.
You'd be making her do
something she's obviously
afraid to do, and that's
talking honestly with her mom
and dad. And they still won't
have enough money.

ALLISON

Wow. Well, okay. It was just my
first idea. My brain is a
little plugged up. Let's look
at our loyal subject's
responses. Maybe they'll
surprise us.

BONITA

(reading over her shoulder)

I think they missed your point,
Princess Allison. One thinks

the world would be a better
place if skateboarding was our
Number 1 priority. Another
believes dogs rank higher than
parents. That weird guy who
calls himself *Nerd2Beat* sent us
half a page of math
calculations.

ALLISON

What do you suppose he means by
that?

BONITA

(giggling)

Dunno. Maybe happiness equals
math? We get some strange stuff
sometimes.

ALLISON

It's just harder for Princess
Allison to help Sophia with her
priorities when it looks like
our loyal subjects haven't a
clue about theirs either.

BONITA

You know, Princess Allison, it
really doesn't matter what our
loyal subjects have to say.
You're the one we all listen
to. You're the one who counsels

us. So maybe it will be up to only *you* to fix Sophia. And if you haven't any ideas, then maybe you'll have to ask for help.

Scene 3

Aqualine and Bonifay exit the Castle, perusing the fresh proclamation and rolling it as they walk.

AQUALINE

It seems that ever since I raised the discussion on our magic stretchy substance, my loyal subjects have clamored for more details on its development. I know our royal alchemists, and a baker, are working day and night to develop this creation for our kingdom. Stretchy could mean riches for whomever discovers it. But I personally think the true riches will come to whoever fashions my Gators.

BONIFAY

They could be vast.

AQUALINE

My excitement doth overwhelm my

heart.

BONIFAY

What's that ahead, Princess?

AQUALINE

It looks like a scuffle. Oh
dear, why do you suppose they
are shouting?

*As Bonifay and Aqualine draw nearer, the
shouts continue.*

TOWNIE 1

I have the secret potion! I
will win!

TOWNIE 2

You? How could am imbecile like
you hope to claim victory? I am
an alchemist!

BONIFAY

Here, princess, let us seek
shelter in St. Timothy's.

*They push the door into the church, where it
is quiet.*

SIR MICHAEL

(Startling the girls)

Little Princess Aqua, are you
here for your prayers?

AQUALINE

Oh my!

SIR MICHAEL

Did I frighten you, little
princess?

AQUALINE

Yes, brave knight, you did. But
alas, not so much as our
townsfolk outside. I fear I
have erred.

SIR MICHAEL

Oh, brave princess. You take
upon your young shoulders such
wise and reaching endeavors.
But your youth prevents the
guidance your loyal subjects
need right now to quiet them.

AQUALINE

What dost thou suggest?

SIR MICHAEL

You have ignited the
imaginations of the realm and

that is indeed laudable. Yet
the virtuous move amidst
rascals and wayfarers and your
challenge to create *Stretchy*...
pardon my efforts with this odd
name.

AQUALINE

I labor to find it's betterment
but so far, we have dubbed it
Stretchy.

SIR MICHAEL

You desire to create this odd
substance, but it has had
consequences that you did not
foresee. Confusion and fist
fighting as now. Yet, say, I
have an idea! Yay, a grand
idea, indeed. We will hold a
festival and judge our
alchemists' concoctions. You
will see, my little Princess
Aqua, that with your wisdom and
my might, together we will
serve and protect your realm.

*Princess Aqualine and Sir Michael put their
heads together, whispering.*

Scene 4

*At Home. Hallway and Kitchen. Allison and
Bonita are by the railing and Mom and Mike are*

sitting at the kitchen table.

MOM

(calling from table)

Allison! Bonita's mom wants her home. And it's time for dinner!

ALLISON

Ughh. Time to go, Lady Bonita. We'll work on this tomorrow.

BONITA

How should I act tomorrow in Gym?

ALLISON

Like regular. But I'd be prepared for Sophia to act a little stranger to you than usual.

BONITA

Do you think she might actually talk to me again?

ALLISON

Yeah, she might. But just in case, don't get your feelings hurt if she doesn't. Sophia doesn't want people to know she has a problem, remember?

BONITA

Yup. I gotta go. Your mom's lasagna smells too good. It's killing me.

ALLISON

(walking into kitchen, talking to audience)

My mom's lasagna is the best, and she makes it for *me* as a special treat. But whoa, look whose here. Mom hadn't said anything about Mike coming over for dinner. I haven't seen Bigfoot since the other night. But there he is, sitting in the chair at the head of *our table*. Just look at his enormous legs bulging forth beneath the wooden top. And Mom next to him, dishing *my* special lasagna onto *his* plate!

MOM

Hi, honey. Mike has a stake-out tonight, so I thought it would be nice if he would stop by for dinner first.

ALLISON

(to audience)

Just look at him and that red beard! He's smiling at me with those enormous white teeth. He actually looks kinda cute. Oh no! He's lifting his fist again!

MIKE
Yo, Princess. Kids rule!

(kissing mom's cheek)

Fabulous lasagna, honey. Come and sit with us, Princess. Tell us what's going on in your world.

ALLISON

(to audience)

Whoa...no way! Who does this guy think he is? Part of the family? It would serve them both right if I just ran back upstairs. But maybe I shouldn't for two reasons. First, I haven't thanked him yet for my pink scarf and my fuzzy journal. I need to be polite. Princess Allison would be very critical of any behavior that wasn't at the very least, polite. My *second* reason is that I am amazingly hungry.

183

MIKE

(winking)

Come on. Sit. Eat. You think too much for a kid.

ALLISON

(sits down at the table)

(to audience)

So, okay. I'll sit down but I might throw up. Mom has that goofy expression on her face whenever she looks at him. All silky and smiley and happy. And she's giving him entirely too much of my lasagna!

MIKE

You usually this quiet?

MOM

Oh, she's just a little tired from school and her nightly webcast. How'd it go tonight, honey?

ALLISON

(to audience)

Now they're both watching me

like I'm a baby, about to spit
up. Waiting for my words to
upchuck onto the table.

(to Mom)

It was okay. So, who are you
staking out?

MIKE

We've got a couple guys
planning a bank robbery. Caught
them on video a couple weeks
back robbing the Third Savings
Bank downtown. We got a tip
saying they're planning to take
down another bank tomorrow
morning. We want to catch them
in the act.

ALLISON

Wow. What would they do to you
if they found out you're there,
watching?

MIKE

(chuckling)

Well, Princess, we're pretty
good. We don't plan to be
caught. We plan to catch *them*.
But, in answer to your
question, they probably would
just call off their plans. Lay

low. Pretend they were planning
a trip to the beach and not a
bank heist. There wouldn't be a
shootout like you see in the
movies, if that's what you're
wondering.

ALLISON

(to audience)

That was exactly what I was
wondering. If police work was
as dangerous as we kids see on
TV, I figure there wouldn't be
many police around. They'd
either be dead, or their kids
would have convinced them to
take a job as an accountant or
Wal-Mart store manager, or
something else less risky. Hey
now, maybe this could be an
idea for a Princess Allison
webcast. *Meet the Real Police...
the Police are our friend...*

Pretty lame titles. What had
Bonita said the other day? That
Mike reminded her of *Thor*. But
not all police looked like
Mike, so a program called
Police—The Modern-Day Thor
wouldn't be good. Maybe a
knight in shining armor? Now,
where had that idea come from?
Police as modern-day knights.
Now, that's a good title.

MIKE

You're thinkin' too much again,
Princess.

ALLISON

I've got a...well, let's just
call her a friend, who's in
trouble. Her family is out of
money and her brother needs an
operation and they don't have
insurance. She's come to me.
Well, she's come to *Princess
Allison the Benevolent* for
help. And I'm not sure what to
do for her.

MOM

(coming over to hug Allison)

Oh honey. I'm so sorry for your
friend. I figured there might
come a time when you'd be asked
to solve something tougher than
footwear issues.

ALLISON

Mom, the *Gators* segment was
very popular. It's like
Princess Allison the Benevolent
has only existed in the web
world. She hasn't had to really
do something before.

MOM

I disagree. She's helped kids
make the right decisions and do
the right thing. Those are
really big things.

ALLISON

I guess I hadn't realized you
understood.

MIKE

I have an idea. Let's put on a
fund raiser for the sick kid.
My department does it all the
time. We can hold it at the
fairgrounds. We can charge an
admission, have games and
rides. Sell food and baked
goods that folks have donated.
Even have a raffle. All the
money goes to pay for the
operation. The whole police
force shows up. Radio stations
promote it and the community
comes out. It's great.

ALLISON

Would that really work? Would
they really do it?

MIKE

(winking at Allison)

Stop thinkin' so hard,
Princess. Problem solved.

Scene 5

*Allison's bedroom. She is making her webcast.
Bonita sits next to her.*

ALLISON

My loyal subjects, *Princess
Allison the Benevolent* here to
tell you about a great event
happening next weekend at the
LaPoste fairgrounds. It's a
fund raiser for one of our
realm who is in dire need of an
operation. Now, as you can
imagine, his family doesn't
want everyone to know that
they're broke and can't afford
this operation, so we're
keeping his name a secret. But
trust your Royal Princess that
your support and participation
in this fund-raising fair is
very important. So, tell your
friends and bring your family.
It will be great fun and every
penny is going to this very
worthy cause.

Princess Allison herself is
going to be very busy for the

next couple days coordinating this event with my new friends at the LaPoste police department. These police are such wonderful protectors of our community. If we were all living five hundred years ago, these guardians would be known as the Knights of our Kingdom. And it is for this reason as well as my personal obsession with the Renaissance that we're making this a Renaissance fair. So, come out Saturday and eat some turkey legs and cake. My Queen mother is making her famous lasagna. Trust me, that it is a mouth-watering treat! See you all there! *Princess Allison the Benevolent signing off.*

BONITA

I'm hungry. You're talking too much about lasagna. This is going to be a great event, Princess Allison. I'm proud to help, and once again, to be your Lady in Waiting.

ALLISON

Wow. Thanks Lady Bonita.

BONITA

And you seem to be patching things up with Mike. He's working really hard on this fair.

ALLISON

You're right. I'm starting to call him Sir Michael.

BONITA

Really? Is that another character from the Renaissance?

ALLISON

Uh-huh. Sir Michael the Moral was a huge knight who helped *Princess Aqualine the Wise* accomplish her great deeds. They were a great team, but they didn't get along well at first, either.

Scene 6

Aqualine reads her proclamation to Lady Bonifay in the town square. Townspeople meander by.

AQUALINE

Dear loyal subjects of the kingdom of LaPoste, Princess

Aqualine the Wise issuing her proclamation on the eve of our great festival. History will credit the winner of tomorrow's judging for developing this amazing substance, that we will only temporarily dub Stretchy. With dry feet and dry houses, my loyal subjects will live longer and prosper.

Special thanks to Sir Michael the Moral for this glowing solution and for his assist to plan this festival. My mother, the Queen, will be the honorary host for this judging. Our kingdom's chief wizard will be the head judge.

Come one! Come all to the town square festival tomorrow. Tell your friends and bring your families. Princess Aqualine the Wise wishes you a good day.

BONIFAY

If you'll pardon the suggestion, Princess Aqualine, but I believe that this competition is a bit out of hand.

AQUALINE

Come walk with me now, Lady

Bonifay, and we will post this proclamation. If perchance we find Sir Michael, perhaps he will calm our concerns.

A villager runs up.

TOWNIE 1

Yay, Princess! I can't wait for our Gators. Look at my shoes here. These are all leaky.

AQUALINE

My Goodness. The sole is flapping away from your leather boot. I don't believe we'll have anything developed in time to replace those! You'll need to find a cobbler, sir.

BONIFAY

Oh no, Sarafina is coming. Princess Aqualine, I worry her purpose.

AQUALINE

Lady Bonifay, I too worry. Perhaps the Princess in my Head has conceived something too large for our realm. And as you say, I have allowed our loyal subject's expectations to soar, perchance to crash.

Nonetheless, we must meet Lady Saraphina with graciousness.

SARAFINA

(breathless)

Princess Aqualine, I am happy to find you. Have you another proclamation?

BONIFAY

For you to scoff?

SARAFINA

Oh no. Have I ever scoffed, truly? My father has dispatched me to find you herewith. He believes he has concocted your Stretchy! I have not seen him so full of life for many years. He has been so sad. Our fortunes changed and he was required to farm but he is not a farmer, he is a mixologist. My mother sang your praises just this morning with special thanks for igniting his spirit and perhaps doing great good for the land. When I told of what great friends we were, she sent me right away to confirm the arrangements for the fair.

BONIFAY

Sarafina, I do not recall your friendship...

AQUALINE

Lady Bonifay. Let us embrace our loyal subject as we have met a need in her family, as well as one within the realm. Sarafina, help us post my proclamation with the details to tomorrow's fair. I will speak with Sir Michael and insure your father a prominent position right up front where he can dazzle the alchemists and judges.

BONIFAY

Do your fellow ladies...

SARAFINA

My pack?

BONIFAY

Well, yes. Do they know of your father's interest?

SARAFINA

I confess they may have their reservations, but to see the joy once again in my father's

countenance to mother's and
mine is like the heavens
opening. I know Father will
win. I just know this...

AQUALINE

Our best luck and wishes to you
and your father. Until
tomorrow...

*Sarafina departs. A great whinny is heard and
Sir Michael enters.*

SIR MICHAEL

(laughing)

Dost he frighten you Princess?

AQUALINE

(laughing)

No, perhaps not. But he used
to. Both you and your horse did
when I was a little girl. But I
am much older now.

BONIFAY

We see you as a modern-day
Thor. A defender of our realm.
And one on whom we can count
tomorrow.

SIR MICHAEL

Thor. I like that. It is my great red beard, no doubt.

AQUALINE

Thou are more than a marvel.

BONIFAY

If you will pardon the correction, Princess Aqualine, there is no such *more than a marvel*. There is only a marvel.

SIR MICHAEL

Either way, I am pleased. Worry not about tomorrow's festivities. Your realm will respond. We will have your winner *and* we will have a remarkable invention!

Sir Michael exits and a boy walks up to take his horse.

ACQUALINE

And who doth you be?

YOUNG HAROLDSON

(*bows*)

I am page to Sir Michael and soon to be Knight of the realm.

AQUALINE

Methinks not *that* soon.

YOUNG HAROLDSON

They call me Haroldson, as I am
the son of Sir Harold.
Princess, if you will pardon my
query, why dost thou worry so?

AQUALINE

Ah, Sir-To-Be Haroldson, some
perceive me as silly and I
worry that it may be true. That
if my marvelous idea fails, I
will never be more than a
Little Princess of Privilege
who contributed nothing to her
realm.

YOUNG HAROLDSON

Mi'lady, you need not trouble
yourself on this. You are brave
and wise beyond your years.
Your inspirations are odd, but
so helpful. They have inspired
me to be braver than my nature:
to think of how I may serve my
realm, and not only how I might
serve myself. I am honored to
serve you.

He bows. Aqualine blushes. They exit.

Scene 6

At the Fair. One side is modern day. The other side is Renaissance. The characters intermingle. Allison and Bonita gather.

BONITA

Princess Allison, may I present you with a perfectly grilled turkey leg?

ALLISON

This drumstick is as thick as my wrist.

BONITA

My mom and I cooked them to perfection.

ALLISON

These are *yours*?

BONITA

We made up four platters of turkey drumsticks for today's fair. I convinced her that every kid needed good quality protein in their diet. Even kids like me with a few extra pounds. She listened to our

food pyramid webcast and
*Princess Allison the
Benevolent's* advice. Then she
consulted with my pediatrician.

ALLISON

Instead of her personal
trainer?

BONITA

Exactly. An expert on
children's nutritional issues.
And, voila! We shopped
together, and I helped her
cook.

ALLISON

Why didn't you tell me earlier?

BONITA

You've been really busy with
Mike and his police buddies,
setting things up for the fair.
Besides I wanted to surprise
you! You and Mike are getting
along really well now, right?

ALLISON

Yeah, he's really great.

BONITA

But he still doesn't get this
Princess Allison thing yet,
right?

ALLISON

He's catching on.

BONITA

Liar! No, he's not! He got you
that shirt you're wearing
today! I just know it! It's
pink and sparkly and says, "I
am a Princess."

ALLISON

Nah, he just wanted all my
loyal subjects to be able to
recognize me.

BONITA

Yeah, right! Did you ever thank
him for the fuzzy journal and
the pink scarf?

ALLISON

Yup. I'm using the scarf as a
bandana. And Mom has the
journal up at the reception
table, taking everyone's name
as they come in. Let's go see
how she's doing.

Walks back among clowns in police uniforms,
little kids, circus tent, Police officers in
jeans and t-shirts bearing the LaPoste Police
Department (LPD) insignia served up the plates
to moms and dads and kids streaming through
the line.

ALLISON

(walks up to a table to buy)

Wait—I want to get Mom a cup of
coffee and a Blondie. How much?

POLICE OFFICER

No way, Princess. You made this
all happen. Your stuff is free
today.

ALLISON

How cool. Look at the line—
there must be hundreds of
people here!

MOM

(to lady in line)

No, we don't know the name of
the boy who will get the
operation. His family wants to
keep it all a secret, so we're
respecting their wishes. My
boyfriend Mike is on the Police
force and he's going to have
the check presented to the

family through my daughter
here, whose been coordinating
it all.

Allison walks up to them.

LINE LADY

So, you must be *Princess
Allison the Benevolent*. My son
listens to your program every
night. He convinced me to get a
better computer set-up so that
he could. He follows your
rules. He's very well behaved
now and much more considerate
of his younger brother. We
still have trouble with him
writing math equations all over
the place, but I figure he'll
grow up to be another *Einstein*.

BONITA

OMG! Our weird loyal subject
Nerd2Beat has a mother!

*Pack girls pay admission and enter, swishing
hair.*

SOPHIA

(*paying admission*)

Hello, Mrs. Warner. It's good
to see you again.

MOM

Well, hello Sophia. I'm happy
to see you coming out for a
good cause. It's been a long
time. How's your mom and dad?
Your brother?

SOPHIA

They're okay, I guess. Ooohh,
here's Allison. I need to say
hi to her.

MOM

You *do*? Well then, say hi to
your mother for me. She and I
were friends when we lived in
the old neighborhood.

SOPHIA

I remember.

*Sophia joins Bonita and Allison under a tree.
Sophia is choked up and starts to cry.*

SOPHIA

I can't believe this. All these
people coming out. And look at
those amazing costumes.

(points at Renaissance girls)

My brother's going to be okay

now. I just know it. And the
most amazing part is that you
kept our secret!

ALLISON

I know. It was tough.

SOPHIA

I told my mom.

BONITA

Oh my gosh!

SOPHIA

I told her that I'd come to
Princess Allison for help and
that you and Officer Mike had
planned this great fair to
raise funds for Jason. I
thought she was going to blow
up. But instead she just sat
down on the bed and cried.
We're a lot alike in that
regard. We cry a lot. Then she
hugged me, and then she ran
into my brother's room and
hugged him. She had been really
worried. She's a good mom.
Really, she is. Sometimes she
gets her priorities mixed up,
but I think she's seeing things
more clearly now.

BONITA

What will she tell your dad?

SOPHIA

I don't know. Maybe she'll say
that she found the money. I
don't think she'll tell Daddy
the truth.

ALLISON

(hugging Sophia)

Your world is so complicated.
Trying so hard to look perfect.

MIKE

Hey Princess! Wait up!

Policemen jog beside Mike, holding two ropes
dragging something. They part to reveal a
wheel chair with a smiling Jason inside.

SOPHIA

Oh my gosh! Jason!

JASON

Hey Sophia! These guys are so
cool. I can't believe they put
this whole thing on for me!
It's incredible! Hey Princess
Allison! You do good work!

ALLISON

Are you talking to me?

JASON

Yeah, you in the pink shirt. I
know who you are. I remember
shooting hoops with your dad.

SOPHIA

Jason—how did you get here?

JASON

I rode with them...

*Sophia's mom and dad come up behind police
officers.*

SOPHIA

Mommy and Daddy!

BONITA

I guess this is a private
moment. Since no one is paying
attention to me, I'm going to
sneak into the food tent for
some cotton candy.

ALLISON

But I thought you were all into

protein?

BONITA

There's just so much of that a body can stand. You can't expect me to change overnight!

(curtsying)

My most highness *Princess Allison the Benevolent*, you have today proven you are deserving of your name and your reputation. It is an honor serving you as Lady in Waiting.

Mike and his police buddies, and Sophia's family look on as Allison helps Bonita to her feet. They push fists into the air.

ALL

Kids Rule!

Renaissance Side of Fair. Aqualine and Bonifay walk forward.

AQUALINE

Oh, my goodness. I believe Sir Michael and the panel of judges have declared a winner.

BONIFAY

Look to see what a wonderful

event Sir Michael has created
and all for *you*.

AQUALINE

And lest we forget, my loyal
subjects, each alchemist
displayed immense knowledge of
how this odd substance *Stretchy*
could be applied within our
kingdom to improve our lives.
Everything from covering wagon
wheels, to storing food, to
blanketing crops against cold.
And lest we forget to mention,
Gators.

BONIFAY

How fared Sarafina's father?

AQUALINE

Lord Michelin and Lady
Saraphina are over there, near
the judges. Let us away to see.

SARAFINA

(hugs her father)

Oh Father! Oh Father! This is
indeed a happy day. You have
won!

LORD MICHELIN

But alas, I have not colorful
offerings. The only footwear I
could mold turned out
black-and-white.

*(holds up a crude model of a
Gator striped black and white)*

AQUALINE

My Gators are colored as a
Zebra? How wonderful! Lord
Michelin, I believe that
history will credit you with
this triumphant invention!

LORD MICHELIN

History will credit you, also
Princess Aqualine.

AQUALINE

And Sir Michael the Moral, too.

BONIFAY

Yes, and Sir Michael too, for
providing this vision and
direction. I am truly honored
to serve as your Lady in
Waiting.

*Bonifay curtsies and struggles to get up.
Aqualine and Saraphina assist.*

BONIFAY

Whew! I am terribly sorry, Princess. These winter months I have added too many new pounds to my already ample figure. I am afraid I am getting fat!

AQUALINE

Lady Bonifay, let me tell you about an idea that came to me in my dreams a few nights ago. Have you ever heard of something entitled the *food pyramid*?

They walk away into the fair. Curtain falls.

The End

J. G. Matheny

PART III
The Musical

THE PRINCESS IN MY HEAD

To create a musical version of *The Princess In My Head*, adapt "Part II: The Screenplay" by inserting the musical numbers into the script as indicated below.

ACT ONE

SCENE ONE
"TOGETHER"
(Duet with Aqualine and Allison)

SCENE TWO
"EDICTS"
(Duet with Allison and Bonita)

SCENE SIX
"SARAPHINA'S BALL"
(Group Number with Saraphina and Town Youth)

SCENE EIGHT
"I KNOW THIS"

215

(Duet with Bonita and Richie Harrell)

SCENE NINE
"SECRETS"
(Sophia Solo)

ACT II
SCENE ONE
"CONFIDENCE"
(Aqualine Solo)

SCENE TWO
"WAITING"
(Allison Solo)

SCENE FOUR
"DO THE RIGHT THING"
(Duet with Allison and Big Mike)

SCENE SIX
"LOVE & PROTECT"
(Duet with Princess Aqualine and Sir Michael)

SCENE SEVEN
"FINALE: KIDS RULE"
(Cast and Chorus)

Visit www.ThePrincessInMyHead.com for music, lyrics, production tips and inspiration.

THE END

About the Author

J. G. Matheny draws from real life to captivate her readers with intriguing story lines, realistic characters and humor. A former journalist and FBI Agent, her first two mystery novels in the Samantha Wilde FBI series drew from her knowledge of bombs, task forces and financial crime. Her middle-grade novel, THE PRINCESS IN MY HEAD, was developed for her daughter to explore resources for problem solving. Her current ventures include an 1892 historical fiction where existing technology and forensic investigation combine to solve a mystery on a west bound train.

Matheny lives with her family in Castle Rock, CO. She holds a Bachelor Degree in Journalism from the University of Wyoming, and a Master Degree in Journalism from New York University. She is currently President for Wyoming Writers, Inc. and a member of Rocky Mountain Fiction Writers. She still works as a financial crimes investigator.

Author website at http://www.ThePrincessInMyHead.com

J. G. Matheny

If you enjoyed *The Princess in My Head*, consider these other fine books from Aignos Publishing

The Dark Side of Sunshine by Paul Guzzo
Happy that it's Not True by Carlos Aleman
Cazadores de Libros Perdidos by German William Cabasssa Barber [Spanish]
The Desert and the City by Derek Bickerton
The Overnight Family Man by Paul Guzzo
There is No Cholera in Zimbabwe by Zachary M. Oliver
John Doe by Buz Sawyers
The Piano Tuner's Wife by Jean Yamasaki Toyama
Nuno by Carlos Aleman
An Aura of Greatness: Reflections on Governor John A. Burns by Brendan P. Burns
Polonio Pass by Doc Krinberg
Iwana by Alvaro Leiva
University and King by Jeffrey Ryan Long
The Surreal Adventures of Dr. Mingus by Jesus Richard Felix Rodriguez
Letters by Buz Sawyers
In the Heart of the Country by Derek Bickerton
El Camino De Regreso by Maricruz Acuna [Spanish]
Diego in Two Places by Carlos Aleman
Prepositions by Jean Yamasaki Toyama
Deep Slumber of Dogs by Doc Krinberg
Saddam's Parrot by Jim Currie
Beneath Them by Natalie Roers
Chang the Magic Cat by A. G. Hayes
Illegal by E. M. Duesel
Island Wildlife: Exiles, Expats and Exotic Others by Robert Friedman
The Winter Spider by Doc Krinberg

Coming Soon:
Comic Crusaders by Richard Rose

Aignos Publishing | an imprint of Savant Books and Publications
www.aignospublishing.com

The Princess in My Head

as well as these other fine books from Savant Books and Publications

Path of the Templar—Book 2 of The Jumper Chronicles by W. C. Peever
The Desperate Cycle by Tony Tame
Shutterbug by Buz Sawyer
Blessed are the Peacekeepers by Tom Donnelly and Mike Munger
Bellwether Messages edited by D. S. Janik
The Turtle Dances by Daniel S. Janik
The Lazarus Conspiracies by Richard Rose
Purple Haze by George B. Hudson
Imminent Danger by A. G. Hayes
Lullaby Moon (CD) by Malia Elliott of Leon & Malia
Volutions edited by Suzanne Langford
In the Eyes of the Son by Hans Brinckmann
The Hanging of Dr. Hanson by Bentley Gates
Flight of Destiny by Francis Powell
Elaine of Corbenic by Tima Z. Newman
Ballerina Birdies by Marina Yamamoto
More More Time by David B. Seabird
Crazy Like Me by Erin Lee
Cleopatra Unconquered by Helen R. Davis
Valedictory by Daniel Scott
The Chemical Factor by A. G. Hayes
Quantum Death by A. G. Hayes
Running from the Pack edited by Helen R. Davis
Big Heaven by Charlotte Hebert
Captain Riddle's Treasure by GV Rama Rao
All Things Await by Seth Clabough
Tsunami Libido by Cate Burns
Finding Kate by A. G. Hayes
The Adventures of Purple Head, Buddha Monkey and... by Erik Bracht
In the Shadows of My Mind by Andrew Massie
The Gumshoe by Richard Rose
Cereus by Z. Roux
Shadow and Light edited by Helen R. Davis
The Solar Triangle by A. G. Hayes
A Real Daughter by Lynne McKelvey
StoryTeller by Nicholas Bylotas
Bo Henry at Three Forks by Daniel Bradford
One NIght in Bangkok by Keith R. Rees
Kindred edited by Doc Krinberg

Coming Soon:
Navel of the Sea by Elizabeth McKague
Talking Story: Storytelling Meets Phenomenology by Jamie Dela Cruz

Savant Books and Publications
http://www.savantbooksandpublications.com

Made in the USA
Middletown, DE
29 July 2019